Praise for

Monica Burns

"Burns doesn't disappoint!"
— **RTBOOKreviews**

Monica Burns writes with sensitivity and panache.
— **Sabrina Jeffries, NYT bestselling author**

"powerfully done…the scenes between Tobias and Jane mesmerized me. I loved it."
— **Joey W. Hill**

"No one sets fire to the page like Monica Burns."
— **eCataromance**

"Definitely recommended reading."
— **The Romance Studio**

Love's Portrait

by

Monica Burns

Table of Contents

Chapter 1

London, 1892

I t's wicked, Julia. Absolutely wicked!"

Alva's squeal of appalled dismay made Julia Westgard smile with satisfaction. Her friend's horrified cry was an understatement. The painting was more than wicked. It was shocking. She turned back toward the painting she'd commissioned. Tipping her head to one side, she studied it with a critical eye.

The nude painting made her look lush and sensual. Isaac Peebles had managed to make Julia look almost beautiful. Almost, but not quite. Although she did like the way the artist had captured the color of her hair. Her hair was her best feature. On the canvas, soft gold highlights spun their way through dark red hair that tumbled over her bare shoulders. Peebles had said the studio lighting had made her eyes a deep moss green, and the portrait reflected his opinion. The color made her eyes in the portrait far lovelier than the plain hazel ones she saw in the mirror every day.

"I like it." Hands resting on her hips, she smiled with a sense of defiance. Oscar would have been horrified. No. He would have been furious, and her punishment would have been painful. Her fingers dug deep into the silk material, layering Her hips. "I like it very much. Do you think I should hang it in the salon or the study?"

"Good Lord, Julia. You cannot *possibly* be serious!"

The appalled note in her friend's voice made Julia turn quickly toward the petite woman. At the horrified look in Alva's blue eyes, she realized she'd teased her friend long enough. One hand pressed against the dove gray silk of her dress, she shook her head.

"I'm teasing you. Of course, I'm not serious."

The relief on her friend's pale features made her bite down on the inside of her mouth. Actually, she'd been more serious than she realized. She simply didn't possess the bravado to display the portrait. For all intents and purposes, she was a coward. The confident way she carried herself in front of her friends was nothing but a façade. Everything she said and did was a performance to cover up the inadequacies she felt every day. The shortcomings Oscar had regaled her with the entire time they'd been married.

Even though he'd been dead for almost two years, his cruel taunts and behavior had left their mark. Oscar had played the impeccable, caring husband in public. Privately, he'd taken every opportunity to humiliate her. The bedroom had been the worst degradation of all. The inadequate feelings her husband had cultivated in her still ran close to the surface, but since his death, she'd done everything possible to regain her sense of self-worth. It was one of the reasons she'd commissioned the nude portrait. It had been an act of rebellion and an effort to regain the uninhibited joy for living she'd lost during almost ten years of marriage to a brute.

"Ah ha, Calvert *said* I would find you here."

Catherine Dewhurst poked her head into Julia's boudoir. At the lively sound of the woman's voice, Julia moved quickly to embrace her cousin. Of all her in-laws, Catherine had been the only Westgard to show her kindness when she'd married into the family. The two of them had found themselves married to men of a similar nature, only Catherine had been freed several years before Julia. Of all the people she knew, Catherine was the only one who could see beyond Julia's false façade.

"Come see what arrived this morning." She grasped Catherine's hand and pulled her cousin toward the painting.

"Is it here? Finally?"

Julia nodded and smiled widely as Catherine stepped around the easel to stare at the completed canvas. Instantly, color flooded her cousin's cheek before laughter parted her lips.

"*Dear Lord, Alva.* However, did you manage to keep from fainting?"

Clearly affronted by the suggestion that she was incapable of surviving a shock, Alva's pale face took on a pinched look. "I'm not a simpleton, Catherine, I've seen nude paintings before, but this one is not in a museum. This is something quite different."

"How is it different?" Julia straightened her back as she prepared herself for her friend's contempt.

"Well…it's you," Alva said as color flooded her face. "You're beautiful, Julia, but why in heaven's name did you have to have the man paint you naked? It's scandalous."

"I don't think it's scandalous."

"Rubbish, it's shocking. Why, the man saw you naked." Alva's straitlaced tone sounded so much like Oscar's. She immediately tossed a pleading glance in her cousin's direction.

"Do try to explain to her, Catherine."

"Perhaps she has a point, Julia. It is a bit…reckless, isn't it?" Catherine sent her a sympathetic look. "I know you wish to free yourself from the memory of Oscar's cruelty, but what if the wrong person saw this? What if the artist talks?"

"Other than the two of you, no one else will see it, and Peebles has been well paid to be discreet."

Julia stalked across the room to the painting and replaced the cloth that had covered it earlier. If she'd wanted an unfavorable assessment of her behavior, she only had to listen to Oscar's voice in her head for that. It wasn't as if she'd gone without a chaperone, she'd taken her maid with her to each and every sitting.

Sitting for Isaac Peebles had offered her a freedom she'd never experienced before. The portrait sittings had been a way of freeing herself of the yoke Oscar had settled on her from the day they were married. She had been the one in control, no one else. With a final adjustment to the cloth she'd laid over the painting, she turned to face her friends.

"I'm sorry you find it in poor taste."

"You misunderstand me, Julia. It's exquisite work." Catherine shook her head and frowned. "I merely pointed out that if it were known among the Set that you…all I meant was that I would not like to see the portrait bring scandal down upon your head."

"There won't be a scandal, because I never had any intention of showing it to anyone else," Julia said in a stilted tone. Of all the people she knew, Catherine was the one person she'd thought would understand why she'd commissioned the portrait. She'd even thought sweet, inexperienced Alva would at least recognize Julia's desire to be reckless, even if only in private. Left at the altar years ago, Alva had rejected every suitor since then and seemed content with her life, but there were moments when Julia thought her friend longed for something more.

"He did manage to get your hair color right, that's not easy to do. Even in the more…" Alva blushed deeply. "…the more intimate places."

The quiet statement hung in the air as Julia stared at her friend in stunned silence. Was Alva actually teasing her about the portrait? She shot a glance over toward her cousin. Catherine's expression was equally astonished. Indignation tilted Alva's pointed chin upward.

"Well, I can be outrageous sometimes too," she huffed, sending them both a sheepish glance as the room exploded with laughter. Julia shook her head as amusement continued to bubble out of her.

Alva and Catherine were her best friends. They were the only two people she could count on to love her, no matter how reckless she was. And of late, she'd been as rash as Catherine had said. Oscar's family had viewed her purchase of shares in St. Claire Shipping as not only excessive, but foolhardy. Her brother-in-law, Albert, had even been bold enough to visit her lawyer and suggest Julia was incompetent.

Fortunately, Mr. Baxter had been the one to suggest she invest in a number of different endeavors, and had quickly sent her brother-in-law on his way. A fact she'd been heartily grateful for as Albert was becoming increasingly annoying in his attempts to influence her decisions. It was a situation she'd created herself. She'd leaned on him far too much in the year after Oscar's death.

She'd stayed in mourning for the requisite time period, but when she'd emerged, it had taken her several more months to find the courage to defy Albert's attempt to control her as Oscar had done. It hadn't been easy, but she'd finally managed to convince Albert that she had no intention of following his guidance in business or anything else. Julia intended to live her life as she wanted without a man to dictate to her.

It was her silent shout against the oppressive life she'd endured with Oscar. Her first attempt to reject the narrow confines of her life was the portrait. The adventure had only made her determined to take more risks and live a life free of someone else's dictates or disapproval.

She was the one in control now—no one else. Julia inhaled and exhaled a deep breath. The question now was whether her friends would support her in this new adventure she had devised. It was for a good cause, and the fact it was even more reckless and daring than having herself painted in the nude made her plan even more exciting.

"If you think the portrait is outrageous, then I'm afraid of what you'll say when you hear what I intend to contribute to the Society's next fundraiser." She turned to her cousin. "Shall we tell her, Catherine?"

"Oh, there's no *we* in this idea at all." Catherine carefully removed the hat from her head, meticulously pushing the hatpin into the peacock feathered plumes that trailed down the back of the accessory. Sweeping the short train of her dark green gown to one side, her cousin took a seat next to Alva to eye Julia with a look of disapproval.

"We're—" She paused as Catherine arched a threatening brow at her. "*I'm* going to acquire a silk handkerchief from Morgan St. Claire and auction it off at the Society for Lost Angels to raise money for the new orphanage."

Alva tipped her head to one side, her expression puzzled. "Well, that doesn't sound all that daring. I'm sure Mr. St. Claire will be happy to part with a piece of silk for the children."

"I don't intend to ask him for the handkerchief. I intend to sneak into his rooms at the Clarendon tomorrow night at the dinner party he's hosting for his investors." Julia smiled at the thought.

She was feeling quite pleased with herself about the plans for her latest adventure. To pull one over on Morgan St. Claire would be almost as pleasurable as when she occasionally found errors in his books. More importantly, it would be a gesture of support for all the women the man had dallied with in the past, then left them with nothing more than a monogrammed handkerchief and a broken heart as tokens of their liaison.

"*Oh my heavens, Julia.* What if he catches you?" Alva sent her a horrified look.

"I have no intention of being caught. I've already made arrangements for one of the maids on his floor to give me access to his rooms and be my lookout."

"But couldn't you just ask him for the handkerchief? He's such a gentleman, I'm sure he won't refuse your request."

"Please, Alva, do *not* give her the opportunity to address Morgan St. Claire's faults." Catherine grimaced at the other woman. "We'll be here all day listening to her rail at the man's shortcomings."

"But Mr. St. Claire is said to be most charming," said Alva in a bewildered tone.

Julia glared at Catherine before she turned back to Alva. "Morgan St. Claire is a scoundrel of the worst kind who thinks nothing of tempting a woman into sin then leaving them heartbroken with nothing but a handkerchief as a memento of their affair."

She frowned slightly. That wasn't completely fair of her. After all, she'd only heard rumors about the man's behavior. Julia knew better than to take the stories at face value. But on the other hand, she'd been on the receiving end of St. Claire's charm when he'd thought to circumvent her determination to review his books. Just yesterday, he'd teased her about wanting to learn everything she could about the shipping business.

"And your antipathy towards the man makes me wonder why you chose to invest in his company?" Catherine eyed her mockingly.

"Business should never be guided by emotions. St. Claire Shipping is a sound investment."

"I see." Catherine's ironic reply earned her a look of puzzlement from Alva and a glare from Julia.

St. Claire Shipping had been an excellent investment. Armed with Baxter's list of candidates, she'd selected four different ventures, including the shipping company. If Albert or any of the other Westgards were to discover she was actually reviewing accounting ledgers and conducting business in person with St. Claire, the family would immediately close ranks in an attempt to control her, just as her husband had. Perhaps they would have good reason in this instance.

Morgan St. Claire. A shudder rippled through her at the mere thought of the man. He'd been the one drawback to her investing in the company. Although she'd never met St. Claire until her purchase of shares in the shipping magnate's holdings, she was quite familiar with the man's reputation.

But it wasn't until she met him that she understood why so many women fell at his feet. Morgan St. Claire wasn't just handsome. His sinful dark looks were like a fierce storm threatening to tear her asunder. All the more disturbing were those piercing blue eyes that saw everything, yet revealed nothing. There was an air about him that commanded obedience.

And he definitely didn't like his authority being questioned. Particularly when it came to her examination of his business accounts. Something she'd done a great deal of over the past few weeks. Even she'd been surprised by her daring when she'd insisted on reviewing the company's books before she invested her money.

Although she'd trusted Baxter's recommendations, she'd wanted to learn more about the businesses she'd chosen to invest her monies in. Initially, St. Claire had been stubborn in his refusal to grant her access to his accounting and clerks, but when she wouldn't budge on the issue, he'd begrudgingly agreed.

The fact that he'd conceded defeat in the face of her persistence had amazed her. Morgan St. Claire was a man who gave commands. He didn't take them. And his concession had bolstered her confidence more than anything else she'd done since Oscar's death. It had helped ease the feelings of worthlessness her husband had cultivated in her. But more importantly, it had given her a confidence she'd lost on her wedding day.

Oscar had controlled her every move during their entire marriage, and that she'd found the wherewithal to stand up to Morgan St. Claire illustrated how far she'd come in such a short time. St. Claire was used to getting his way, but she'd stood her ground with him and won. The small victory had fortified her confidence, and strengthened her resolve never to let any man control her ever again.

"I still don't see why you find it necessary to sneak into the man's hotel room instead of just asking for a handkerchief." Alva's obvious disapproval pulled Julia out of her thoughts.

Frustrated, she shook her head. Didn't either one of her friends understand why she needed to do this? Her actions would have appalled Oscar, and that alone was enough to make her do it. But it also gave her the opportunity to provide the Society for Lost Angels with an item that would fill their coffers. She had no doubt that there was more than one woman willing to pay handsomely to own a St. Claire handkerchief, if only for the notoriety of its original owner.

"Because, Alva, it won't have as dramatic an impact if I ask him for one. Sneaking into the man's hotel room and taking a handkerchief without getting caught will cause a stir among the ladies. They'll want details about his hotel room, which I'll be happy to elaborate on as long as they bid on the blasted thing."

"Surely you're not about to confess to any member of the Marlborough Set that you entered the man's room?" Alva looked askance at the idea.

"Of course not." With a wave of her hand, Julia smiled patiently at her friend. "I'm simply going to explain that the woman who took the handkerchief prefers to remain anonymous. For obvious reasons, of course."

"Of course." Catherine coughed her disparagement, forcing Julia to glare at the woman.

"I'll tell everyone the woman took the handkerchief on a dare and agreed to let me share the tale of her nerve-wracking adventure."

"I think it's far too dangerous, Julia. Surely there has to be some other way to acquire the man's handkerchief." Alva frowned in obvious disapproval. "Catherine, she'll listen to you. Tell her it's a mistake to even attempt this."

"I've already tried," her cousin said in a disgruntled voice. "I can't reason with her."

"Because you've not been able to tell me that my plan won't work." Julia eyed Catherine with irritation. "I'm taking every precaution, and it's something I *have* to do."

Julia wasn't altogether sure why this latest scheme of hers was so important. It just was. The only genuine risk with having Peebles painting her had been trusting him not to show the canvas to anyone. The man had an impeccable reputation for discretion, and she'd paid him well to keep the portrait a secret. There had not been even the slightest hint of rumor regarding her sittings, which made Julia certain the man had kept her confidence.

But the entire time the man was painting her, she'd experienced an exhilaration that had been intoxicating. Maybe that was why her plan to steal St. Claire's handkerchief was so important to her. She wanted to experience that sensation again. The pleasure of doing something wicked and getting away with it.

The portrait had been a simple adventure. Taking a handkerchief from St. Claire's room was much more risky. Frighteningly so, but Julia wanted to test her newfound courage to be even more daring. Of course, she wasn't sure how courageous it was to undertake what was a rather foolhardy venture. But she'd made up her mind and refused to back down now.

"But how will you prove that it's really Mr. St. Claire's handkerchief?" Alva's brow puckered as she was clearly trying to find holes in Julia's well-laid plans.

"His monogram. We've all heard the story of how he gives a handkerchief to each of his mistresses as a parting gift when he breaks with them." Julia grimaced at her words. "Supposedly for the woman to dry her eyes."

She had no idea if the story was true or not, but she wouldn't put it past Morgan St. Claire's arrogance. The man was a well-known womanizer, and she understood why. As much as she hated to admit it, the shipping magnate had a dizzying effect on the senses.

"Oh, that sounds so romantic."

"Don't be a ninny, Alva. It's not romantic at all." Catherine turned her glare on Julia. "As for you, cousin, I think you've gone mad. You'll cause a sensation if you're caught, and there's the distinct possibility of being ostracized. You know how the Queen is about circumspect behavior. Although, as far as the Prince of Wales is concerned, Bertie would probably applaud you. Still, polite society won't overlook an outright discretion of this sort."

Julia waved her cousin's concerns aside. "I won't get caught. I have it all planned out. Dinner is being served in St. Claire's private dining room at the Clarendon tomorrow night. I'll simply ask to refresh myself, then run upstairs and retrieve the handkerchief from the man's room. I'll be back at the dinner party before anyone is the wiser."

"What is that old adage? The best laid plans go astray?" Catherine's mouth was tight with disapproval, but there was concern in her gaze too.

"My maid knows the maid on St. Claire's floor. The girl is quite trustworthy. I promise you. Nothing will go wrong."

Julia smiled at both of her friends with a sense of extreme satisfaction. Nothing would go wrong. She was certain of it, and she was going to enjoy auctioning off one of St. Claire's handkerchiefs. She would be the first woman to own one that *hadn't* been given in a moment of pity.

Chapter 2

Morgan St. Claire caught the faint aroma of citrus on his left as he reached for his wine glass. Every muscle in his body was tight with expectation. A sensation he'd not been able to rid himself of from the first moment he'd seen Julia Westgard's portrait. Head tilted to one side, he listened half-heartedly to Edward Parkinson drone on about his race horses, while Morgan studied Julia out of the corner of his eye.

The rich-colored blue of her gown enhanced the warm peach tone of her skin. She was like a tempting dessert he wanted to keep all for himself. His gaze lingered on the rounded top of her breasts and the dark cleft between them. Although he couldn't see them, he knew her nipples were a deep mauve color.

His cock stiffened slightly at the thought of Julia's portrait. Ever since his first glimpse of the painting, it had kept him awake more nights than he cared to admit. Particularly when Peebles had snatched the cloth from him and hidden Julia's nude body from view before Morgan had even had time to appreciate the artwork or its subject.

It had been quite by accident that he'd even seen Julia's provocative portrait. Morgan had visited Peebles's studio to view a painting of a friend. As always, Jonathan had been late, and while waiting, Morgan had inadvertently dislodged the material over Julia's portrait. The partial view had been so entrancing he'd exposed the rest of the portrait despite Peebles's outrage.

The fact that the artist had refused to offer up any information regarding his subject had been frustrating. Morgan had even hired a street urchin to watch the artist's studio, but the boy had provided him with nothing useful in his attempts to find the woman in the portrait. It made him think Peebles had warned the lady of Morgan's interest and other arrangements had been made with regard to her sittings.

Morgan had been stumped as to how to find the subject of Peebles's painting, and when Julia had walked into his shipping office near the docks, he'd been rendered speechless. He was never at a loss for words, but it had taken him several minutes to gather his wits when she'd arrived with her lawyer to discuss investing in his company. The woman in the portrait had been that of a sensual, sultry woman accustomed to pleasing a man and enjoying the same in return. But the Julia who'd entered his office was vastly different from the woman he'd imagined.

In fact, she was a challenge. With her cool exterior and impervious resistance to Morgan's flirtations, she only managed to increase his determination to reveal the woman he'd seen in the portrait. With an understanding nod in Parkinson's direction to indicate he empathized with the man's problems, Morgan turned his head to look directly at Julia.

She was still engrossed in conversation with another of his investors, and it afforded him the opportunity to study her profile for a moment. She wore her auburn hair up, leaving her slender neck exposed while revealing the delicate shape of her ear. His mouth went dry at the thought of nibbling at the spot where her neck met the gentle indentation of her shoulder. A wisp of hair had broken loose from her upswept hair and brushed against her soft-looking skin. He almost reached out to touch it, but caught himself in time.

Damnation, he needed to control his fascination with her. One way or another he intended to have Julia Westgard in his bed, but he wasn't about to let his cock lead him about like a dog on a leash. Morgan's lust for the woman had already made him break one of his most important rules. Never mix business with pleasure. Until Julia, it had never been an issue. He knew it had been a serious error in judgment to agree to let her invest in St. Claire Shipping, and yet before he could stop himself, he'd agreed to sell her shares in his company.

Morgan's jaw tightened. His agreement to the contingencies she demanded as part of her investment had been even more egregious. It was one thing to consider indulging in a liaison with the woman, but to open up his office doors to her was altogether a different matter. And yet, Mogan had done just that. He'd agreed to let the woman experience his company's operations first-hand. A fact that illustrated how fascinated he was with the woman. And he'd do well to remember where enthrallment generally led.

It was a well-known fact that his mother had supposedly captivated his father in the beginning, and Morgan knew how well their marriage had turned out. His throat closed up slightly. It hadn't taken Morgan's father long to stray from his wife. Embittered by the man's blatant affairs, his wife had come to hate the sight of Morgan because he was a younger version of his sire. Between his mother's distaste for him and his father's indifference, Morgan's childhood had been less than pleasant. And the experience had done little to recommend the state of matrimony to him.

Julia reached for her wine glass, and the movement interrupted the unpleasant retrospection of his childhood. Beneath his gaze, Morgan saw the pulse in the side of her neck flutter. The delicate movement indicated she was aware of his stare, and from the rigid set of her shoulders to the way her fingers curled around the stem of her wine glass, her tension was plain to see. Morgan enjoyed knowing he unsettled her. It meant she wasn't immune to him.

He stared at her lips for a long, drawn out moment. It was a tempting mouth. The wine had stained her lips a dark red, and a sudden urge to taste her latched onto him with all the force of a charging bull. He fought the desire clamping down on every inch of his body as he watched her take a bite of her salmon. Despite her attempt to present a calm composure, he knew she was anything but.

"You seem distracted, Mrs. Westgard." He bit back a smile as she jerked her gaze up to his, then just as quickly looked away.

"Do I?" There was a catch in her voice before she regained that serene composure she'd consistently displayed since their first meeting. "Forgive me. I'm simply savoring this delicious salmon. The hotel's chef has outdone himself. Do you suppose he would send me the recipe?"

"Actually, I have a personal chef who prepares all my meals, and I'm afraid Henri refuses to share his secrets." Morgan deliberately paused and offered her a secretive smile. "Even with me."

"What a pity." She took another bite of her dinner, and Morgan's gut tightened as he watched her mouth and suddenly wished they were alone. Her throat flexed slightly as she swallowed. "This salmon is a dish I could eat quite often."

"Then come back for dinner again, next week," Morgan said as he leaned toward her, his voice dropping a level so that his invitation reached only her ears. The startled expression on her face made Morgan smile, and he saw Julia's hand tremble as she quickly laid down her fork.

"I think that would be unwise. One should never mix business with pleasure."

He bit down on the inside of his mouth at having his own rule thrown back in his face. She was right, but it was too late to go back now.

"Perhaps." He reclined back into his chair and lifted one shoulder in a shrug. "Although I'm sure it would be quite—pleasurable."

Julia immediately took another drink of her wine, this time more a gulp than a sip. If possible, her confusion made her even more beautiful. What would Julia be like if she were slightly inebriated? Relaxed and uninhibited, with no barriers between them. The thought was a pleasurable one.

"I'm glad to see you're enjoying my Bordeaux." He grinned as a pink flush crested in her cheeks. She shot him a baleful look, which only made him chuckle as he lowered his voice even more. "You blush quite charmingly, Julia."

"I don't recall giving you permission to call me by my given name." Her back ramrod straight, she attempted to stare him down with a haughty expression. It did little good, and he flashed another wicked smile in her direction.

"No? Forgive me, I thought you had."

There was nothing remotely apologetic in his response, and they both knew it. She toyed with the necklace at the base of her throat before she tightened her mouth and met his gaze directly.

"Well, I didn't, and I prefer to keep our relationship strictly a business one."

"And if I don't?" he challenged with a smile.

Chapter 3

Julia swallowed hard at the way the man almost purred the words. Sweet mother of God, the man's reputation was well earned. Morgan's gaze was a sensual caress as he scanned her features before it moved downward to her bodice. The warmth of a flush filled her cheeks at the blatant stare of interest. No, not interest—insolence, that's what it was. He was being insolent.

Morgan had been far from happy with her demand to observe his shipping operations. Even the suggestions she'd made for improving different processes in his offices had been met with little more than a dark frown or grunt of irritation. Julia had been a thorn in the man's side for the past few weeks, and now she was paying the price for daring to challenge the great St. Claire.

His gaze held hers as he reached for his wine glass, and the knot in her throat thickened at the way his fingers stroked the stem of the crystal goblet. Taking his time, Morgan drank from the glass, and all the while, his movements kept her mesmerized. A secretive smile curved his mouth, and he arched an eyebrow at her.

Flustered and embarrassed that she'd been staring, Julia jerked her gaze back to her plate and resumed eating. With her head bent, she didn't see him lean forward, but she felt him and drew in a quick breath.

"You haven't answered me, Julia."

Dark and spicy, his male scent tickled her nose. An unfamiliar sensation streaked across her skin and sent her heart skidding out of control. Irritated she was acting like all the other women who'd fallen under St. Claire's spell, she clenched her jaw. Fixing a neutral expression on her face, she lifted her head to meet his mocking gaze with her steady one.

"As I said, *Mr. St. Claire,* I prefer we keep our relationship on a firm business footing."

"You're far too exquisite for any man to think of you as simply a business associate, *Julia.*"

The honeyed tone of his voice made her feel as if she were the only woman he'd ever found beautiful. She gave a slight shake of her head. That was ridiculous. This was Morgan St. Claire, the man who gave away his handkerchief whenever he parted company with a lover.

"Are you flirting with me, Mr. St. Claire?"

"Would you like me to?" There was a dark note in his voice, and she shivered.

"No."

"As you wish."

The enigmatic smile on his lips evolved into one of dry amusement as he leaned back in his chair. She tried to avoid drawing blood as she bit down on the inside of her mouth. God, he was an arrogant bastard. Did he really think he had but to crook his finger and a woman would come running? Of course he did. And the terrifying thing was, a small part of her wanted to do just that.

It made Morgan St. Claire a dangerous man. Even men gave way to his persuasive charm. She'd observed him conducting business enough over the past few weeks to realize that. And if the man thought Julia Westgard was going to succumb to his sensual charms just like everyone else, he was wrong. She wasn't about to let any man control her again, no matter how devastating he was to her senses.

Her fingers trembled as she reached for her wine glass again, then stopped. She'd had enough to drink already, and she needed to keep her wits about her. The sooner she secured the item she'd come for, the sooner she could leave.

Without waiting for him to speak again, Julia turned to the man on her left and started a conversation. Anything to avoid conversing further with Morgan St. Claire. Although she couldn't see him watching her, the blast of heat warming Julia's skin told her the man's gaze was still pinned on her.

The effect of St. Claire's intent gaze tightened her muscles and had her poised on the edge of a cliff. If she fell, she wasn't sure where she would land. The thought sent a shiver streaking down her back, and she barely managed to focus on her conversation with the man next to her. Being only one of two women investors in the small party of twelve guests this evening was enough to strain even her own daring. And she found herself wishing Lady Falkenhouse was not at the opposite end of the table.

For the first time, she wondered why St. Claire had placed her on his left. She frowned at the thought. That would imply he'd deliberately chosen her seat. No, she was reading too much into the seating arrangements.

With the meal complete, she and Lady Falkenhouse left the gentlemen to their port. As she left the dining room, the warmth on the back of her neck told her that St. Claire was watching her leave. Immediately, the sensation of hundreds of butterflies milled in her stomach, their wings beating frantically inside her.

Lady Falkenhouse smiled mischievously at her as they entered the sitting room that was part of Morgan's extensive suite of rooms at the Clarendon Hotel.

"I think you've captured St. Claire's attention, my dear Mrs. Westgard," Lady Falkenhouse said with amusement.

"He was being polite." Julia's stomach lurched at the thought of others seeing St. Claire might be interested in her. Might be? The man had made it quite clear he was.

"Bah, the man is besotted with you. He could barely keep his eyes off you all evening."

"I'm sure he was simply being polite," Julia murmured before she sought to make her escape. "If you'll excuse me, Lady Falkenhouse, I would like to freshen up."

Julia didn't give the woman a chance to invite herself along and walked quickly out of the sitting room into the hall that connected all the rooms of Morgan St. Claire's suite. Once in the corridor, she saw a young girl waiting at one end. Aware that the moment of truth had arrived, Julia hurried forward.

"Please hurry, ma'am," the girl whispered as Julia reached her. "I don't want to get caught."

"Neither do I," Julia replied and pulled a pound note from her reticule. The girl glanced furtively over Julia's shoulder before taking the money, then pointed to the door behind her.

"I'll watch the door for as long as I can, ma'am, but I mustn't be gone from the kitchen long. Henri will wonder where I am."

With a silent nod, Julia slipped through the doorway into a darkened room, closing the door behind her. It took several seconds for her eyes to adjust to the low light from the small blaze in the fireplace and the oil lamp on a table between two chairs in front of the hearth. Above the mantle was a painting of the Calcutta, one of St. Claire's prized ships. She paused to admire the framed artwork.

If there was one thing she liked about the man, it was the pride he took in his company and fleet of ships. He might be a seducer, but she knew he had integrity as well. He always dealt fairly with his customers and his staff. Julia frowned. She wasn't here to contemplate Morgan St. Claire's good qualities. She had a handkerchief to find.

With a whoosh of air, she exhaled the pent-up emotions that had been building inside her since she'd left the dining room. For all her bravado, the idea of being caught in St. Claire's bedroom was a terrifying thought.

There would be too much explaining to do, and she didn't think Morgan St. Claire would find her explanation amusing. Despite her apprehension, she experienced the familiar rush of exhilaration that always flowed through her just before she was about to take a risk. It was still quite a new sensation, and she relished it.

Blood pumped its way madly through her veins as her gaze swept around the masculine room. It was as sensual in nature as the man who slept here. Heavy drapes framed the large canopied bed, and it was difficult to tell if they were navy blue or black. Gold tasseled cords held back the material, and a spread that matched the curtains covered the bed. The overall impression was an elegant decadence, if it were possible to describe debauchery in such a way.

A small pinprick of guilt made her hesitate. Perhaps she was being unfair to the man. His flirtation with her might be unsettling, but he'd given her no reason to believe he was anything but an honorable man. With a shake of her head, she grimaced. She was wasting time. Dragging her eyes away from the bed, she glanced around for the wardrobe. The enormous chest was across the room, and with swift steps, she crossed the floor to open the doors.

More than a dozen suits filled the massive storage, and she shifted her gaze to the drawers that lined one side of the furniture's interior. The first drawer revealed nothing but cuff links and watch fobs. Closing it, she moved on to the next drawer.

When it didn't offer up the treasure she sought, Julia uttered a noise of frustration. She went through two more drawers before she found the prize she hunted. Triumph sailed through her as she pulled one of Morgan St. Claire's monogrammed handkerchiefs from the drawer.

"It appears you've found one of my handkerchiefs."

The softly spoken observation made her cry out in surprise. Whirling about, she saw Morgan watching her with a narrowed gaze. Arms folded across his chest, he studied her in silence. The quiet thickened and weighed down the air in the room until it was difficult to breathe, let alone manage to speak. Julia swallowed the fear threatening to close her throat. Dear Lord, how was she going to explain what she was doing in his room?

"I…I'm sure this must look terrible to you, Mr. St. Claire. But it's not what it seems, I can assure you."

"I'm listening."

He was listening. Of course he was. The question though, was what to tell him. The truth. She could tell him the truth. No, he'd never believe her. If Julia were him, *she* wouldn't believe her story. Stealing a handkerchief to auction off at the Society for Lost Angels would sound too fantastic, and he would immediately label it a falsehood.

"I…I was curious…I mean, I wanted to know…umm…I wanted to have one of your handkerchiefs." Her response made him arch an eyebrow, while his expression was filled with skepticism.

"I see."

When Morgan didn't move, Julia sucked in a quick breath, suddenly conscious of the fact she was trembling. At least he hadn't asked her to return the silk square of material she held in her hand. The best thing to do was flee. That is if she could make her feet move. She took one step toward the door before he blocked her way.

Julia had never seen a man move so fast or so silently before. It was disturbing. He not only barred her path, but he was inches away from her. Having him stand so close set Julia's pulse pounding even faster than it had when he'd surprised her only moments before. Dear Lord, what if he took her appearance in his bedroom as a sign she was interested in him? No. She'd made it clear that a liaison between them was out of the question. She bit her lip at the realization that her current circumstances did little to help support that position. Her fingers twisted the handkerchief in her hand as she struggled to keep her wits about her.

"Surely, you're not leaving so soon." Morgan's voice was as smooth as the silk she held in her hand.

"I…I've been terribly rude and ungracious in the face of your hospitality, Mr. St. Claire. I am deeply sorry."

"There's no need to apologize, Julia."

"That's generous of you to say, but I truly regret my intrusion into your private domain. If you'll step aside, I'll rejoin your other guests." It was a struggle, but Julia experienced a moment of satisfaction that she'd managed to regain her composure.

"And leave me to fend for myself?" The suggestive remark sent heat flooding into her cheeks. Despite his slight smile of amusement, she knew he wasn't happy to find her in his bedroom.

"You're forgetting your guests."

"I'm certain they're managing quite nicely without us."

"Without us?" she exclaimed. Dear lord, she'd forgotten that as one of only two women in attendance tonight, her absence would not go unnoticed.

"I explained that an important business matter required my immediate attention, and that I would return momentarily. It won't take them long to realize we're both missing. They'll quickly come to the conclusion that my urgent business matter involves you."

Morgan's soft voice was almost a tangible caress against her skin. Julia tried not to shiver, but as she met his gaze, it was impossible not to shudder with trepidation. The man was eyeing her in the same manner a wolf does its supper. She frowned for a brief second before her stomach lurched violently.

"But everyone will think—"

Appalled, she struggled to suppress the panic rising in her throat. His gaze unreadable, he folded his arms across his chest.

"I'm not in the habit of caring what others think."

"Naturally. But at the moment, it's not your reputation in jeopardy," she snapped.

"Perhaps you should have considered the risks more carefully before visiting my room."

She winced at the hint of steel in his voice. He was right. Julia had been so certain it would be a straightforward task to steal a simple handkerchief. She'd been wrong, and it was incredibly irritating to have to admit that he was right. Well, there was little she could do about having been caught. What mattered now was extricating herself from the current situation.

"As much as I hate to admit it, you're correct Mr. St. Claire. I erred in my risk calculation. I apologize for intruding. Now if you'll excuse me, I'll rejoin the others."

In a quick movement, she tried to skirt him, but he was faster. Once more, he blocked her way, but this time there was practically no space between them. Heat radiated off Morgan's hard, muscular body, and the strength of it created a frisson across her skin that alarmed her. She swallowed her dismay as she met his penetrating gaze.

"You've yet to explain why you need one of my handkerchiefs, Julia."

The way he said her name sent dozens of butterflies fluttering about in her stomach. There was an intimate, possessive sound to it, and she wasn't quite certain what it meant. Worse, Julia didn't like the delicious sensation that skimmed down her spine.

One thing was perfectly clear to her. The resolute line of his lips said Morgan wasn't about to let her leave the room until she'd given him an explanation for her behavior. Julia clenched her jaw in frustration.

"If you must know, I wish to auction off the silk at a luncheon for the Society for Lost Angels. We're trying to raise money for a new orphanage."

"And you think my handkerchief would draw a large sum?" Morgan frowned with dark skepticism.

"Yes, I do," Julia said with indignation. "Unfortunately, there are a number of women who think it romantic you offer your lover a handkerchief with which to dry their tears when you break with them."

Morgan studied her with that mesmerizing gaze of his for a long moment before he smiled. It was a smile of dangerous charm, and Julia sucked in a sharp breath at the power it held over her.

"And you don't subscribe to the idea that it's romantic."

"No, I do not."

"Interesting, although I'm still not convinced any of your Society's members will buy this small trifle."

She trembled as his fingers glided along the side of her forearm before flicking the silk square she held tightly in her hand. Even through her evening gloves, his fingertips singed her skin. The amused skepticism in his eyes infuriated her. The man knew little about the women in the Society. The handkerchief she held would bring a tidy sum to the orphanage fund.

"Shall we make a wager on that, Mr. St. Claire?" she said through clenched teeth. His gaze narrowed at her biting tone.

"Hmm, an interesting notion. What do you propose we wager?"

A shiver of trepidation skated down the length of her spine. God in heaven, she was as reckless as Catherine said she was. But she was in the pond now. There was nothing for it, but to swim for shore with what little decorum she had left.

"If I sell the handkerchief to one of the Society's members, you must offer up an equal sum for the orphanage fund."

Folding his arms, he arched an eyebrow. "An intriguing wager. So if you sell my handkerchief to one of these women at auction, I'm to offer up the same amount as the sale price?"

"Correct." For the first time since their conversation began, she relaxed. She would still escape with the means to increase the orphanage's finances.

"Since you've laid the foundation for this wager, I think it only fair that I be allowed to name *my* terms if I should win."

"Of course." Julia smiled at him with a touch of self-satisfaction as she waited to hear his condition of the bet.

"Very well. My terms regard a portrait I saw quite recently. I've not been able to forget the woman in the painting, and I want to see her reclined in my bed, a willing participant in a night of passion."

The soft edge in his voice raised the hair on the nape of her neck. The glint of triumph in his brown gaze held a hint of something else that made her struggle to swallow the fear and apprehension threatening to squeeze her throat closed.

"I don't understand. What portrait are you referring to?"

"It was an exquisite portrait, erotic almost. In fact, just looking at it made my cock spring to attention."

The shocking words made her gasp, but words of protest failed Julia. She could only stare at him with a sinking feeling of horror as he offered her a wicked smile.

"Let me see if I can describe the woman in the portrait. She was quite beautiful. Her hips were softly curved and voluptuous. Her full mouth was parted in a seductive pout. And her breasts were full and succulent looking."

"Oh dear God." The words parting her lips were barely audible as she stared at him in horror. He was describing her portrait. How had he seen it?

"Then there was her hair—it's a beautiful color. Not quite red, not quite brown, even the nest of curls between her legs is the same delectable color."

Instantly, Julia's cheeks blazed with heat at the wicked note in his voice as he described the more intimate details of her body as Isaac Peebles had painted her. But where could St. Claire have seen, let alone known about, her portrait? Peebles had given his word he wouldn't show the painting to anyone. A shudder shot through her, and Julia clenched her fists as she struggled to maintain a dignified composure.

She wouldn't go through with it. She'd return Morgan's bloody handkerchief and leave his room with at least her reputation intact. No. That was impossible. If Julia backed out now, he'd be insufferable.

It would be unbearable dealing with the man when it came to her financial investment. No, she had to see it through. Morgan might have seen the portrait, but it was in her possession. She had nothing to fear in that area. More importantly, he couldn't win this wager. She'd make sure Catherine or Alva would bid on the silk. After all, as long as one of the ladies in the Society of Lost Angels bought the handkerchief, she'd win.

"This woman in the portrait, do I know her?"

Julia tilted her chin at a proud angle, hoping to convince him she didn't have an inkling as to what picture he was describing. A small squeak of surprise escaped her the moment he tugged her into his arms. Heat enveloped Julia, while her heart raced with excitement despite her desperate efforts to slow the mad pace of its beat.

A muscular arm curved around her waist, pressing her into the solid muscle of his tall frame. His mouth was so close to hers she could smell the expensive wine on his breath. For a fleeting moment, she wondered what it would be like to taste that liquor on his tongue. Shocked by the traitorous way her body was behaving, she braced her hands on his chest and tried to push away from him.

"Surely you will not deny that you have the most delicious looking mocha nipples, Julia. I haven't been able to stop imagining what it would be like to suck on them."

His fingers skimmed over her skin along the lower edge of her bodice. The touch made her mouth go dry at the sudden longing that gripped her. What would it be like to be Morgan's lover? Immediately, her mind careened to a halt. Dear Lord, she needed to keep her wits about her where this man was concerned. She needed to finalize this wager and flee with what little dignity she still possessed.

"I don't deny anything, St. Claire. But if you think you can win this wager, I dare you to accept."

"So you agree that if I win, you'll recline yourself on my bed." The confidence in his expression and voice sounded alarm bells in her head, but she was in too deep to stop now.

"It is easy to gamble when the outcome is certain to be in one's favor, Mr. St. Claire."

"Then let us seal our agreement."

The sudden heat of his mouth against hers caught Julia by surprise. Firm and sensual, Morgan's lips possessed hers with a hunger that made her stomach flip with excitement. It was like being engulfed by fire. As his tongue swept into her mouth, she relaxed into him, unable to prevent her body's wild response to his touch. Hands rough with calluses scraped over her sensitive skin as he cupped her face. It was a kiss of seduction, possession, and mastery all in one.

Her body reveled in the experience, all the while her head was scrambling for clear thought. Rough fingers trailed down to the base of her throat, while a long finger slid under the edge of her bodice. A wave of sensation swept over her at the touch, and her nipples grew hard as her breasts swelled and tried to push their way out of her corset.

Sweet heaven, no wonder women fell at the man's feet. His touch was like a drug. As he deepen their kiss, it drowned out everything but the need for him not to stop. She found herself clinging to him with abandon, while strong, rough fingers undid several buttons at the back of her dress. In protest, she tried to push away, but her gown slipped off one shoulder before she could free herself.

One tapered finger slid its way between her skin and corset, and she gasped as he gently eased her breast up so her nipple popped over the edge of the snug fitting garment. An instant later, he lowered his head and flicked his tongue over the taut bud. The action singed her skin, and she uttered a soft cry of delight the moment his teeth gently clamped on her and tugged at the nipple playfully. The world shifted beneath her feet.

"Please…" Her voice evaporated as he began to suckle her breast. The pleasure spiraling through her veins was indescribable. Moist heat gathered at the apex of her thighs. A moment later, she wondered what it would feel like for his hand to touch her intimately. The picture shimmering in her head shocked her.

Wrenching herself out of his arms, she backed away from him. He looked completely unfazed by their embrace, and she was certain she looked disheveled and disconcerted. In the back of her mind, she knew all too well that the only reason she was free was because he'd been willing to release her.

Embarrassed, she adjusted her clothing with great speed all the while fully aware of his dark eyes watching her. It was disturbing. Even more so because deep inside, she liked the way he watched her. The way he'd touched her. Shaken by the knowledge, she struggled to regain her composure. Her gaze flashed toward him only to see him smiling at her, desire flaring in his eyes.

"I shall enjoy having you in my bed, Julia."

His quiet confidence should have frightened her. Instead, it infuriated her. Her senses restored somewhat by Morgan's arrogance, Julia glared at him. "I think not, Mr. St. Claire. You forget I hold the upper hand."

Sweeping around him, she raced from the room with the sound of his laughter trailing after her. It made her heart lurch with an intense excitement she didn't want to feel, but the sensation spread its way through her body like a raging river. It made her want to return to his arms and experience the delight she was certain she'd find there. Dear Lord, if only she were that daring.

Chapter 4

Today was the day. Morgan threw his walking stick out in front of him with a quick flick of his wrist as he walked, letting the cane briefly touch the ground before it swung outward in another clean stroke. He did it with the same smoothness with which he always pulled on the oars of his boat when rowing on the Thames. Today, Julia Westgard would have to admit defeat when she failed to sell that bloody silk handkerchief of his in her Society's auction.

His cane hit the sidewalk with a small crack of noise, and he frowned. What the devil was wrong with him? He'd never been this enthralled with a woman before. What was so special about Julia that had him tied up in knots? He grimaced. That was an easy question to answer. It was that damn portrait that had gotten him into this infernal mess.

He could have easily found several other investors to make up for the sizable capital she'd put into the business. Even his solicitor had been surprised by the addition of Julia Westgard's name to the investor list. Women were rarely allowed to invest in his businesses. And certainly not young attractive ones. He'd had far too many women eye him as marriage material, and he had no intention of falling prey to that condition. He knew all too well what havoc that institution could wreak.

As a child, he'd learned early on that houses were filled with nothing but discord. It was why he chose to live at the Clarendon Hotel rather than purchase a townhome. Morgan had no wish to be reminded of his childhood. Besides, the hotel suited his needs well. It also eliminated the possibility of a mistress thinking there was anything permanent in their relationship. And it was exactly why Morgan had made it his habit never to do business with a woman unless she was well beyond marrying age.

Now he'd broken that unwritten rule, and he was paying for it. He must have been insane to let the woman invest in his company. No, simply blinded by lust. A desire that would have faded eventually if not for the day Julia had crossed the threshold of his office. The moment she and her solicitor had entered his offices on Beckton Road near the docks, he'd lost his ability to think straight.

The woman Morgan had seen in the portrait at Peebles's studio had been hidden behind a serene façade. Without realizing it, Julia had silently challenged him to break through that aloof, reserve of hers. Not even when her solicitor had outlined the stipulations tied to her purchase of shares in St. Claire Shipping had Morgan thought twice about accepting the offer.

In agreeing to let her review the company's books and learn how his company operated, Morgan had practically salivated at the opportunity it presented. He'd made it his goal to charm his way into her bed, no matter how long it took. When Morgan had discovered her in his bedroom fleecing one of his silk handkerchiefs, he'd taken full advantage of the situation.

For once, that ridiculous story circulating among the Marlborough Set about his method of ending an affair had yielded something other than his amusement. Several years ago a discarded mistress had started the rumor, and he'd ignored the gossip. Now that falsehood would give him Julia, and when he was done with her, she'd be begging for a second silk handkerchief.

Morgan paused as he reached the stoop of Lady Eldred's town home. Pulling his pocket watch out, he clicked the timepiece open. Excellent, just in time for the auction. Lady Eldred had taken great care to apprise him of the Society's meeting schedule and had agreed to keep his impending visit a secret. Julia was about to have the surprise of her life. He smiled as he strode up the steps and used the brass knocker.

The door opened immediately, and he handed over his hat, gloves, and cane to the butler. From the partially open salon door, he heard Julia's voice ringing out. It was a melodious sound. But then everything about her was pleasing, right down to the way the pulse on the side of her neck throbbed erratically when she was in his arms.

He slid quietly into the room to take a seat in the chair Lady Eldred had told him she would save for him. Julia's attention was focused on one of the Society members, and he was pleased Julia failed to notice his arrival. From his seat in the back of the room, he watched and waited.

"So you see, ladies, this handkerchief is available to the highest bidder today. Think of it. This silk square belonged to the notorious Morgan St. Claire, and it was procured under the most harrowing circumstances."

"Exactly what were these excruciating conditions, Mrs. Westgard?"

"Start the bidding with twenty pounds, Lady Plumpton, and I'll tell you."

He watched the woman in question nod her head in agreement. Julia's radiant smile made him suck in a sharp breath, and his cock stirred in his trousers. Damn, but the woman was an enticing witch.

"Thank you, my lady. I have twenty pounds—do I hear forty while I share with Lady Plumpton as to how I came by this silk square?" Julia turned back to the first bidder, her mannerism far from the restrained woman he was accustomed to seeing in his shipping office. "First, I must tell you that I'm sworn to secrecy not to reveal the identity of the friend who acquired this infamous handkerchief."

"I bid thirty pounds, Mrs. Westgard." A matronly woman raised her hand to bid on the item. "How did your friend acquire the handkerchief? Is it from one of St. Claire's discarded lovers?"

"Thank you for your bid, Mrs. Fellowes. No, this item was not given freely. It was taken right from underneath the great man's nose itself. My friend, who shall go nameless, entered the lion's den, simply to acquire this handkerchief."

"Good heavens! Do you mean your friend…oh my word." Mrs. Fellowes went silent, and Morgan leaned slightly to one side to see the woman's face become beet red. Immediately, he suppressed a chuckle at the way Julia was embellishing her story.

"I bid fifty pounds if you tell us what lion's den, Mrs. Westgard," said a timid looking young woman on the front row.

Julia, hazel eyes shining with mischief, moved to the other side of the room and smiled at the bidder. Folding his arms across his chest, he bit back a grin. The minx was enjoying keeping these women on tenterhooks.

"Thank you for that bid, Miss Alverton. In fact, the lion's den was no other than…" Julia paused for effect. "Morgan St. Claire's very own bedroom at the Clarendon."

The collective gasps in the room merely widened Julia's smile, and her mischievous pleasure made it difficult for him to restrain his laughter.

"Oh no, Mrs. Westgard…surely not." The woman called Miss Alverton shook her head in horror.

"I'm afraid so, although my friend confessed it was a frightening adventure."

With a dramatic gesture, Julia held up his handkerchief for inspection. "As you can see, here are the illustrious initials of the man himself. So which of you lovely ladies dares to own a genuine Morgan St. Claire handkerchief? All without having succumbed to the man's licentious charms?"

Her blithely spoken words made his muscles tense with annoyance. Licentious. The woman was about to find out just how unrestrained he could be in the bedroom, and he'd make damn sure she was begging for more before he finished with her. Relaxing back into his seat, he studied Julia's lush, voluptuous figure.

He knew what hid beneath that modest gray dress of hers. His eyes narrowed as he watched her continue to encourage the bidding for the handkerchief. The snug material of her gown clung with seductive longing to her breasts. The pattern slid downward to a pointed vee, just below her waist, before the material covered her hips in a graceful swag to the bustle behind her.

The image of her portrait entered his mind, and he visualized exactly what that vee was pointing too. A nest of reddish-brown curls lay beneath that meek gown, and he had every intention of exploring the velvety folds those curls covered—and soon.

"Do I have any more bids ladies? I have a hundred pounds from Lady Plumpton, do I hear a hundred twenty?"

"Two hundred pounds."

He watched as the sound of his voice reached her. The color drained from her face as she finally caught sight of him in the rear of the room. For a long, dramatic moment, the room was fraught with a loud silence that only sheer astonishment could create. Seconds later, a bevy of excited whispers erupted in the room with dozens of eyes fixed on him. He ignored all the occupants in the room except for one.

"I…Mr. St. Claire…I…I don't think this auction is open to bidders outside of the Society for Lost Angels."

"I see." Morgan arched his eyebrows before shifting his attention to his hostess. "Lady Eldred, I was given to understand that my bid would be welcome today, did I misunderstand?"

Slowly rising to his feet, his gaze sought and met Lady Eldred's mortified expression. His hostess's plump face flushed with embarrassment, and he watched the older woman rise to her feet and nod.

"Yes, Mr. St. Claire, I did tell you we'd be delighted to have you bid at our auction. I…I failed to mention this to you before the meeting started, Mrs. Westgard. I do apologize, my dear."

The woman turned toward Julia, whose face resembled a statue. Despite her lack of emotion, the anger in her tight smile was more than evident. It was evident she'd just realized the trap she'd walked into with her wager. The stipulation had been that one of the ladies in the Society of Lost Angels needed to buy the handkerchief at auction.

Morgan had upset the apple cart by appearing at the auction. Not only was he not a woman, he was not a member of the Society. He could almost see her brain working on a way to escape the trap into which she'd stumbled. A trap he had no intention of allowing her to escape.

"Well then, Lady Eldred, Mrs. Westgard, since I'd like to bid on this item, I repeat my bid of two hundred pounds."

With an almost imperceptible shake of her head, Julia jerked slightly as she rejected his bid. The moment he smiled with satisfaction, her dismay became a glare of outrage. Christ Jesus, she was beautiful when she was angry. And she wasn't just angry, she was furious. His smile broadened.

"Two hundred pounds, Mrs. Westgard. Do I hear any other bids?" He glanced around the room, enjoying the looks of shock and curiosity on the faces of the women surrounding him.

"I bid three hundred pounds."

Confidence glowed from Julia's features again as she made her own bid for the handkerchief. Head tilted at a stubborn angle, Julia met Morgan's gaze with a silent warning not to outbid her. The muscle in his jaw twitched as he gritted his teeth and forced a polite smile to his lips. He had no intention of letting the woman elude him.

"Four hundred."

"Five." Julia's crisp response made his muscles tighten with irritation. Damn the minx. If she thought to outbid him, she was mistaken.

"One thousand," he said quietly.

"Two thousand."

The sharp note in her voice made it clear they were at a stand off. She was hell bent on saving herself from the wager she'd made with him. Her anger was almost tangible as he narrowed his eyes to study her. No doubt, she'd continue to outbid him until she was penniless. But he had no intention of letting her win. In fact, he intended to teach her a harsh lesson. No one—*no one* ever stole from or cheated Morgan St. Claire.

"Before I make another bid, Mrs. Westgard, if I may, I'd like to view the merchandise."

Without waiting for her agreement, he skirted the chairs in front of him, moving along the side of the room until he reach the front row where Julia was standing. As he drew near, her body was no longer supple and relaxed. Her stance was as rigid as a brick wall.

Morgan extended his hand and waited for her to drop the silk square into his palm. Although her face was serene, he saw her fingers tremble as she gave him the auction item. Bending his head, he pretended to study the handkerchief.

"You seem determine to win our wager, Julia, but I have no intention of losing," he murmured, before lifting his head to study her strained expression. "Shall I continue bidding or do I explain how you really came by this handkerchief?"

The sharp inhalation of her breath indicated his words had struck home. He turned toward the waiting members of the Society.

"Ladies, I'm thoroughly convinced this is indeed my handkerchief, and I offer up a bid of five thousand pounds."

He turned his head to look at Julia. The defeat was evident in her gaze. But it was the look of vulnerability in her hazel eyes that tugged at him. It was a disturbing sensation. Julia drew in a deep breath before forcing a smile to her mouth.

"Sold to Mr. St. Claire for five thousand pounds."

The moment her words faded in the air, the room filled with the loud buzz of conversation. Watching Julia, he frowned. He should be feeling elated right now. He'd won. She would be in his bed soon.

A sharp pang of regret rocked Morgan, and he drew in a quick breath at the startling revelation sweeping into his head. He wanted Julia to come to him willingly, not bought and paid for like a whore.

"Bloody hell," he muttered. Her eyes and face empty of emotion, she nodded her head at him.

"You've won our wager, Mr. St. Claire, and I am at your disposal. What time and where am I to present myself?"

The cool mask of detachment on her face angered him even more. The problem was—he wasn't angry with her. He was furious with himself. When in the hell had he suddenly taken to bedding women who didn't want anything to do with him? And there was no doubt Julia had no desire to further their acquaintance.

Teeth clenched in frustration, he studied her in silence for a long moment. Beneath his gaze he saw the veneer of her cool composure crack slightly. No, he refused to bed a woman who was unwilling. But damn it, his body still wanted her.

Suddenly, Morgan realized he needed to use a different strategy where Julia was concerned. Deliberately, he offered her the most charming, gentlemanly smile he possessed.

Hazel eyes flashed with first surprise and then a guarded expression. He gave her a slight bow.

"Mrs. Westgard, are you planning on attending the St. Claire Fete next Friday?"

"I…yes…as an investor, it's my obligation to make an appearance before the company's employees."

"Excellent. I hope you'll save me a dance then. The party can sometimes be a bit rowdy, but I can assure you, I'll not let you come to any harm."

"I am quite capable of taking care of myself, Mr. St. Claire."

"Indeed." His smile broadened at the flush of irritation that tinged her cheeks as her lips tightened into a straight line. "Well, then. I'll take my leave."

"But I…"

"Yes?" He arched an eyebrow at her, fully aware that she was completely bewildered by his actions.

"I…I thought that…" At her obvious confusion, Morgan nodded slightly, then leaned toward her, deliberately keeping his voice low.

"Our wager still stands, Julia. However, I think we should become better acquainted before payment is made."

"Oh."

"I look forward to our next meeting."

Surprise and puzzlement pulled her mouth into a lovely pout. The sight stirred the beast in his trousers. Damnation, if they were alone—no, he needed to hold a calm and steady course with her. Julia was going to be the most difficult challenge he'd ever faced. But she was a prize he intended to win. With a quick nod, he turned and walked away. Time for a change in plans.

Chapter 5

Morgan threw his pencil down onto the open ledger in front of him in disgust. Leaning back into the soft leather of his office chair, he closed his eyes in pain. Hellfire and damnation, this headache was one of the worst he'd suffered in months. He dragged in a ragged breath as a wave of nausea roiled in his stomach.

He should have gone back to his suite at the hotel an hour ago. The Clarendon's head housekeeper, Mrs. Welkins, always had some of his special tea ready for brewing and he could use the stuff now. The throbbing in his right temple hammered away at him, increasing the level of his pain. The sound of his office door opening was a banshee's wail as the pins squealed in their hinges.

"Whoever you are, get the hell out of here, or I'll cut your heart out," he snarled, refusing to open his eyes as the light made the pain worse.

"I believe you would."

Julia's cool tone caught him by surprise. His eyes flew open to meet her haughty gaze. What the devil was she doing here? Another sharp pain gripped his temple, and he closed his eyes again as he swallowed a groan. God damn it, he didn't want her to see him this way. It made him appear weak, and the last thing he wanted was Julia Westgard thinking that he, Morgan St. Claire, was weak.

"Go home, Julia. I'm not in the mood for any questions today."

"Well, I am. I noticed The Merry Widow's manifest indicated it brought into port a cargo of tea, spice and silk. I was wondering if this was a normal shipment. She's made the same run on other occasions, but in less time."

He didn't give a bloody farthing how fast or slow the Widow was, he just wanted Julia to leave him be before he lost the small breakfast of tea and toast he'd foolishly eaten earlier today. Gripping the arms of his chair, he lurched to his feet.

"Get out, Julia." His wounded roar filled the office and accentuated the throb in his temple. With great effort, he barely suppressed the churning in his stomach. "Get out now or I'm likely to say or do something we'll both regret."

His strength ebbing away, he collapsed into his chair. Eyes closed, he waited to hear the grinding sound of the door closing behind her. Instead, he heard the quiet rustle of taffeta rounding the corner of his desk.

"Damn it, Julia. I told you to get *out*." Even despite the pounding of anvils in his head he heard how feeble his command sounded.

"Hush, it's obvious you're not well." The warmth of her hand rested on his forehead for a brief moment as if checking for a fever. "Do you suffer from migraines often?"

"Yes," he growled.

Her fingers gently stroked his throbbing head. The light touch on his skin could have been a feather, but it was enough pressure to ease his pain a small fraction. Inhaling a deep breath, he released it as Julia's fingers slid through his hair to soothe his scalp. Beyond the door, he heard the noisy workings of his staff. He was grateful for the buffer, but he knew he'd have to traverse through the outer office to reach his carriage.

"You should be at home, resting." The gentle whisper made him catch Julia's hand and halt her healing caress.

"I had work to do."

"And now?"

"Now, I'm going home for some peace and quiet."

Forcing himself to stand, Morgan gripped the edge of the desk to keep from swaying as the pain in his temple lashed out with the renewed strength of a hot branding iron. A quiet noise of disgust flew from Julia's lips. Even without looking at her, Morgan could easily visualized the expression of annoyance he'd seen on her face in the past. Too focused on remaining upright, he didn't bother to verify if his assumption was correct. Her firm hand pressed against his arm as Morgan willed the churning in his stomach to stop.

"Sit down, *now*. I'll order your carriage and call one of the men to help you outside."

"No," he rasped as loudly as his head could bear. "I'll walk out of this office under my own volition. I'm not some weak fool, unable to handle a minor headache."

Julia made a sound that was quite close to a snort. If he'd not been feeling so miserable, he would have smiled at the scornful noise.

"You're a stubborn man, Morgan St. Claire."

"Yes."

"I propose a compromise. I'll order your carriage, and when it arrives, I'll help you reach it safely."

The idea of Julia escorting him to his carriage struck him as exceedingly amusing. No, it was humiliating. But he didn't have the strength left to argue. It wouldn't be the first time he'd let the woman have her way, although there would come a time when Julia would give way to *him*.

"Fine."

Without another word of argument, Morgan sank back down into his chair, then rested his head against the warmth of the burgundy leather as he closed his eyes against the light exacerbating his migraine. The whisper of taffeta echoed in the office as she moved toward the door.

Morgan waited for the squeal of the pins in the hinges. When it came, the sound made him flinch. The throbbing pressure in his temple reinforced its message that he remain still. He complied. If he didn't, he'd never make it out of the shipping office without showing his staff he was nothing more than a weakling.

Deliberately, he focused on slowing his breathing in an effort to ease the pressure in his head. Despite his pain, he must have drifted off for a moment as it seemed only seconds had elapsed before Julia was touching his arm again. To Morgan's surprise, he noted the fact he hadn't even heard the sound of the door hinges grating against his senses.

"Morgan, the carriage is here."

He acknowledged her whisper with a grunt, and deep in the back of his mind, he realized it was the first time Julia had ever called him by his first name. The sweet sound almost made his migraine worth the agony to know a barrier between them had fallen to the wayside. Bolstered by the thought, Morgan rose from his chair without her assistance. Using the desk to hold himself steady, he made his way around the furniture at a slow pace.

"Walking stick."

His rough command was hardly a whisper, but an instant later, she offered his cane to him in silence. One arm around his waist, she allowed him to lean on her as he moved toward the door. It was a pleasant sensation. He'd never had a woman he was attracted to aid him in such a manner. Reaching the door, he took a deep breath and gently pushed her away from his side.

"I prefer to walk without help, Julia."

"And you have the audacity to think me obstinate and foolhardy."

Ignoring the irritation in her quiet voice, he braced himself for the noise about to assault his senses. He straightened his shoulders as he opened the office door. "We can discuss my audacity at another time. Right now, I'm waiting on you to lead me out to my carriage.

She sent him a glare as she swept past him and toward the main door of the St. Claire Shipping offices. As he followed her, his head clerk hurried toward him.

"Mr. St. Claire, I need your signature on some documents."

"Not now, Jeremy."

"But sir—"

"I *said* not now."

Each word resounded in his head with the force of a gunshot. Bile rose in his throat as he brushed past the man and walked toward the front door of the office as steadily as he could. Julia waited for him in the open doorway. The light behind her was blinding. It sent a fierce wave of nausea blasting upward from his stomach into his mouth. Morgan fought desperately to control the sensation.

Beyond Julia's voluptuous curves, he could see the open doorway of his carriage. Determined to maintain his composure until he was in private, he continued forward. It seemed like an eternity until he reached the coach door. With what little reserved strength he possessed, he pulled himself up into the vehicle and collapsed onto the padded seat.

Surprise broke through the throbbing in his body as Julia climbed in behind him and closed the door. To his amazement, she quickly pulled the blinds over the light illuminating the vehicle's interior. He had no time to speak as the carriage suddenly rocked forward. In seconds, the swaying of the vehicle made him lurch forward and retch violently. When he'd finished, he sank back against the leather seat thoroughly exhausted. A softly scented piece of linen dabbed at his mouth. It smelled of lavender.

"You'll be home shortly. It will please you to know that the men simply thought you were in a bad mood. They didn't suspect you were unwell." Amusement echoed in her voice. "I imagine they're accustomed to my being the cause of your irritable demeanor."

He barely nodded his head before leaning into the corner of the carriage and closing his eyes. Any other time, Morgan would have teased her in return, but coherent thought was beyond him at the moment. It had been a long time since he'd been this miserable. Of course, he had no one to blame but himself. All the signs of an impending migraine had been there, he'd simply ignored them.

The most puzzling thing was Julia's behavior. It had only been a few days since she'd lost their wager. Every time she'd visited the shipping office, he'd offered her nothing more than a polite and solicitous greeting. Not once had he tried to tease her or engage her in any congenial conversation. Despite his restraint, the stony façade she presented when they'd crossed paths had been impossible to shatter. It made this gentle, caring demeanor of hers all the more disorienting. And the last thing he liked, aside from migraines, was being confused.

Women never confounded Morgan. He was the one to confuse and disconcert the opposite sex. It had become an art form with him. To be on the receiving end was not a pleasant experience. His head suddenly reverberated with a vicious jolt of pain as the carriage bounced hard from some object or hole the vehicle had hit.

Unable to suppress his groan of suffering, Morgan winced. A second later, gentle fingers clasped his hand in a silent sign of sympathy, and his heart slammed into his chest. He couldn't remember ever having a woman treat him with such compassion before. That it was Julia doing so caused him to experience a small rush of pleasure that almost managed to push its way through his torment. The emotion vanished as the carriage bounced him against the wall of the vehicle once more.

Christ Jesus, would this infernal carriage trip from hell never stop? As if hearing the unspoken curse, the coach abruptly rolled to a halt. Suddenly realizing he had to traverse the hotel lobby, Morgan's stomach churned a protest. Sheer will power was the only reason he was able to stave off another bout of sickness. The warmth of Julia's hand through the kid gloves she wore was a tangible sensation as she squeezed his bare fingers gently.

"Wait here a moment, I instructed the driver to take us to the back of the hotel, and I wish to ensure you have an unobstructed path to your room."

Once more her thoughtful consideration surprised him, but the only reply he could manage was a hiss of air. Julia's warmth left his side, as daylight flooded the carriage's interior. The blinding light lasted only a few seconds before the vehicle's door snapped close with a whispered click of the latch. Morgan's condition was too wretched to know how much time had passed before light filled the carriage again. The hint of citrus filled his nostrils as Julia's hand caught his in a gentle grasp.

"I'm not strong enough to keep you from sinking to the floor if you're overcome by pain, so I've arranged for two of the staff to accompany you to your rooms."

"I don't—"

"Do not argue with me, Morgan. Will power can only carry you so far." Julia's firm words indicated she would brook no argument from him. "Mrs. Welkin reassures me you're well acquainted with the two men waiting to assist you. While your ability to leave your office on your own power was quite impressive, from your present appearance, I sincerely doubt you're capable of a repeat performance."

There was no censure in her whispered words, but there was the distinct thread of humor. If he hadn't been so exhausted, he would have taken the time to make an appropriate retort. Instead, he released a grunt of acquiescence. Slowly, Morgan slid across the seat toward Julia, where she stood in the carriage's open doorway. Fingers locked tightly around the frame of the carriage door, Morgan stepped out of the vehicle.

The fresh air gave him a renewed sense of energy, and he steadied himself against the black lacquered panels of his carriage as he managed not to fall flat on his face. Julia's soft curves pressed into his, her arm wrapping around his waist for support. Morgan shuffled forward the few steps between the carriage and the hotel. He'd just managed to wrap his hand around the doorjamb of the Clarendon's back entrance when he realized he was falling. A bustle of activity exploded around him, and one breath later, he pitched forward into a black hole.

Chapter 6

ulia followed the men carrying Morgan into his suite, then down the hall to his bedroom. As she entered his bedchamber, she saw a young woman drawing the curtains closed, while another maid was lighting several candles.

The room was every bit as decadent as Julia remembered, and a small shiver streaked down her back. The two men Mrs. Welkins had ordered to carry Morgan upstairs were laying him on the bed, and the housekeeper was quietly issuing orders to the two young women.

The efficiency with which the staff moved made Julia believe this wasn't the first time they'd seen Morgan incapacitated by a migraine. She experienced a rush of relief that she'd asked the Clarendon's housekeeper for assistance. Julia had been reticent to do so, knowing Morgan would most likely object to anyone helping him.

It had been a correct assumption as she remembered his handsome features darkening with anger when she'd informed him as to what she'd done. Even though she'd firmly insisted Morgan not argue with her, Julia had been worried he would override her. In fact, she was certain that had been his original intent, but he'd not managed to remain conscious long enough to refuse help.

The man had barely reached the back door of the hotel before he collapsed, and Julia was glad she'd asked the housekeeper for help. She would never have been able to keep him from falling to the floor otherwise.

Removing her hat, Julia slid her hatpin through the plumes jutting upward from the base of the hat's crown, then carelessly dropped it onto a nearby chair along with her gloves. Another maid entered the room carrying cloths and a large bowl of water on a tray, which she set on the table next to Morgan's bed. In minutes, the staff finished their tasks and vanished. As the last maid disappeared, Mrs. Welkins turned to Julia.

"I've ordered Henri to brew Mr. St. Claire's special herbal tea, and I'll have someone bring it up shortly, Mrs. Westgard. He'll be wanting it when he awakes." The hotel's housekeeper looked at her with concern. "Are you certain you don't mind looking after Mr. St. Claire for an hour or so? I don't have anyone I can spare at the moment to care for him."

"I'm happy to help, Mrs. Welkins. My father suffered from migraines, and I'm familiar with what needs to be done."

"Then I'll return a little later to relieve you." With a grateful smile, the woman walked out of the room leaving Julia alone with her patient.

Morgan was still unconscious, and she muttered a sound of annoyance. He would need to be undressed so his skin could breathe. Why in heaven's name hadn't she thought to have the men undress Morgan before they left? Now, *she* would have to do it. Julia's heart fluttered with trepidation at the thought.

Resigned to her fate, she blew out a harsh puff of air, then quickly approached the bed. Praying Morgan wouldn't wake up while she worked, she swiftly removed his shoes, then proceeded to undo the buttons of his trousers. Julia had no idea how she managed, but she removed his trousers without shifting his solid muscular body too much.

The entire time she was sliding his trousers off of him, it was impossible not to marvel at his sinewy thighs and calves. She was certain they would possess the same powerful strength of his arms the moment they were entwined with hers. Julia's fingers brushed across one bare leg, and she inhaled a sharp breath as fire streaked over her skin.

Dear God, even when he was unconscious the man still had the ability to unsettle her. Unwillingly, her gaze drifted up to the apex of his thighs where she saw the outline of his phallus beneath the soft cotton fabric of his underwear. Even covered it appeared as impressive as the rest of the man. Something primal stirred inside her, and Julia's mouth went dry at the thought of giving herself to him.

Appalled at the direction of her thoughts, Julia immediately averted her gaze and resumed the task of undressing him. Not more than a minute later, she lost her focus once more as she unbuttoned Morgan's shirt and it fell open. Amazement caused her to suck in a breath of appreciation. The man wore nothing on the upper half of his body.

It was hedonistic for him to forego an under shirt, but if he hadn't done so, Julia would have been denied the pleasure of seeing the raw masculinity of him. As she stared down at Morgan, her heart slammed into her breast. God help her, but the man was beautiful. Without thinking, her fingertips brushed over his hard muscles in a light caress.

The instant Morgan stirred, she jerked her hand away. Biting back words of disgust at her behavior, Julia forced herself to study him analytically as she debated how to remove his shirt. She would have to lift Morgan's head and shoulders slightly to slide his arms out of the sleeves.

She could only pray he didn't awake before she finished her efforts to make him more comfortable. The entire time Julia was removing his shirt, her gaze continuously flitted downward to the apex of his thighs. In an attempt to divert her thoughts, Julia reached for the blanket someone had left on the bed.

Draping it over Morgan, a voice in the back of her head protested at her having covered up such a wonderful male specimen. She ignored the thought and sank down onto the mattress beside Morgan, then reached for the bowl of water sitting on the night table.

Lavender wafted up into the air, and she dipped one of the cloths into the floral-scented water. When the rag was soaked, Julia removed the water from it with a sharp twist. Gently, she laid the cool, damp cloth across Morgan's forehead. For some reason, it seemed quite natural for her to be here—tending to this man.

Staring down at him, Julia noted his features had lost some of the harsh lines that emphasized his commanding nature when he was awake. At the moment, he appeared defenseless, almost boyish. She was certain Morgan wouldn't like anyone seeing him this way, least of all her. Without thinking, Julia brushed a lock of chestnut hair off his forehead.

Flustered by the action, she quickly jerked her hand away from Morgan. Trembling, Julia remembered how she'd recklessly gambled and lost her wager to this man. Although she wasn't happy she'd lost, Julia knew she would honor her debt. She simply didn't like this cat-and-mouse game Morgan was playing. Julia's heart skipped a beat with frustration and fear.

It had been almost two weeks since the day he'd out maneuvered her and won back his handkerchief for a sizeable sum. Morgan had not called on her or sent a note citing his wish to collect his winnings. While Julia was grateful the orphanage had benefited by her rash behavior, she didn't enjoy the man dragging out his demand for payment. It set her on edge.

Perhaps even worse was how pleasant and cordial he'd been since the Society's auction. God, she'd been a fool for having entered into the wager with him. What she hated the most was Morgan's delay in demanding she pay her debt. His extended silence regarding the topic had twisted her nerves to the point she was jumping at her own shadow. Julia knew the man would inevitably claim his one night with her when she least expected it.

Surprise and the unexpected was a tactic she abhorred. It had been one of Oscar's well-honed skills—the element of surprise was how her late husband had controlled her. That, along with fear and criticism. Distancing herself from the painful memory of her repressive marriage, she refreshed the damp cloth on Morgan's forehead.

The man stirred something in her she'd thought long dead. She bit her lip at the thought. It alarmed her to know she was attracted him. He was a threat to everything she'd fought so hard to achieve since Oscar's death.

With a man like Morgan St. Claire, her independence would be at stake. The man was used to getting his way with everything and everyone in his world. He didn't like to be thwarted. At the same time she'd found him a thoughtful and considerate man. Morgan seemed to truly care about the people working for him.

Especially disconcerting was how he'd taken extra time with her over the past few days explaining how the shipping industry worked. Even when she knew he was irritated by her interruptions and questions, he'd answered her patiently and without condescension. Those two facts alone had attracted her to the man all the more. But she didn't want to be attracted to Morgan St. Claire.

Her fingers tingled from the heat of his skin as she refreshed the damp cloth on his forehead. There was a pinched set to his firm mouth. Even in repose, he seemed in pain. She shook her head slightly at the memory of him walking past his shipping clerks as if he was hale and hearty. It had been nothing short of magnificent.

With a frown, she retrieved another rag and allowed it to soak in the scented water. She didn't want to find Morgan St. Claire magnificent. She didn't want to think about or feel anything for the man. The man was a rake—a dangerous one at that. With his handsome face and silk-edged compliments, it was understandable why women fell at his feet. But she had no intention of being classified a St. Claire woman.

The man might have won their wager, but he would never win her mind or heart. She would see to that. Water droplets wet her palm as she gently dampened Morgan's pale features. There was an intimacy to her actions that disconcerted her. Unwillingly, her gaze drifted down to Morgan's bare arms and shoulders.

His skin had been kissed by the sun, deepening his natural skin tone. Julia bit her lip as her gaze roamed over the length of him. The instant her eyes focused on his beautiful male hands, she remembered how he'd pulled her into his arms the night he'd caught her stealing his handkerchief.

Morgan's lips had seared hers in a passionate kiss unlike anything she'd ever experienced. The memory was so vivid, her fingers flew up to touch her burning mouth. Julia had found his kiss more pleasurable than she cared to admit. It had made her feel wicked and daring, and if she were being honest with herself, she wanted more.

It was the same sensation Julia had experienced when she'd posed for her portrait. Swallowing the knot of confusion that tightened her throat, she shook her head slightly. The man was far too attractive for her peace of mind.

God only knew what would happen to her when he demanded she make good on their wager. Even more disturbing was the fact she might find it almost impossible to avoid succumbing to his charms. Julia winced at the thought. There had to be some way to put an emotional barrier between them.

Her gaze drifted back to Morgan's face, noting the tightness at the corners of his mouth had eased somewhat. The cloth on his forehead was no longer cool, so she lifted it from his head and soaked it again. Replacing the damp cloth on his skin, she was pulling away when a powerful hand gripped her wrist.

Startled, she froze. The last time she'd been held so fast, she'd been tied to a bed while Oscar rutted on top of her. Julia suppressed the hideous memory and fought not to jerk free of Morgan's grasp. It would only arouse his curiosity. Something she didn't want. Julia focused her gaze on Morgan's face and saw his eyes were still closed.

"You may leave now, Julia." His voice was husky, almost hoarse.

"And if I go, who will change the cloth on your forehead?"

"I'll manage."

"I told Mrs. Welkins I'd wait for her return."

Stubbornness had to be this man's most annoying trait. She glared at him, mentally challenging him to open his eyes and look at her. He didn't. Instead, his index finger rubbed against the inside of her wrist in the manner of a blind man. The simple gesture filled her belly with fire. His eyes still closed, the corners of his mouth tilted up in a slight smile.

"As soft as I've imagined."

"Stop that." She tried to tug herself free, but his grip simply tightened around her wrist. It startled her that she didn't feel panic at his restraint. If anything, her only fear was that she found his touch far too pleasant.

"I like the feel of your skin beneath my fingers."

"I care little for what you like, St. Claire. Release me this instant," she snapped as the fire spreading across her skin only exacerbated the fear inside her.

"Ahh, there it is again, that waspish tone." Morgan relinquished his hold on her, and Julia stumbled to her feet. She watched him slowly open his eyes to meet her gaze with just a hint of the irreverent mischief she was accustomed to seeing whenever his eyes met hers.

"Whatever are you referring to?"

"You get defensive whenever you're frightened."

"I do *not*, and I am *not* frightened." Julia scowled at the way Morgan's mouth twitched with amusement. It was obvious her lie had been less than convincing. "I think you're right. I should leave. If you're well enough to mock me, then you're well enough to care for yourself."

With one last glare in his direction, she wheeled about and walked stiffly toward the chair where she'd left her hat and gloves. She'd only taken a few steps when a loud crash, mingled with a weary oath of frustration, filled the air. Whirling around, she saw Morgan flop wearily back into the mattress. At the foot of the nightstand, the bowl of lavender water lay in pieces on the floor. Annoyed by his bullheadedness, she returned to the bedside and adjusted his pillows none too gently.

"You, Morgan St. Claire, are the most obstinate man I've ever met. One of these days, that pride of yours is going to cause you to fall flat on your face." Straightening, she scowled down at him with her hands on her hips.

"Your confidence is one of the most intriguing things about you, Julia. I like a confident woman in my bed," he murmured. His observation stunned her. How on earth could he possibly think she was confident? She was the least self-assured person she knew.

"I am *not* in your bed, St. Claire."

"But you will be, and quite soon, I think." His words were soft, almost as if he were talking to himself.

"Then collect your damned prize and leave me be." Julia turned away, only to feel the warmth of Morgan's hand on her wrist once more.

"You are definitely a prize, my sweet beauty, but I'll collect my treasure at a time of my choosing, not yours."

Despite the pain furrowing his brow, his dark brown gaze held a possessive gleam that set her heart pounding like a blacksmith's hammer against an anvil. Mesmerized, Julia stared down at Morgan, knowing the reckoning between them was inevitable. She flicked her tongue out to wet her dry lips, and his eyes narrowed with an emotion that alarmed and exhilarated her in the same breath. Good Lord—she was far too attracted to this man. Heaven help her if she became involved with him. The man would control and manipulate her until he tired of her, and then where would she be? Lost.

Her gaze fell on his fingers holding her fast. The sudden image of her hands bound in a black necktie made her shudder. She'd lived that hellish existence while Oscar was alive. He'd been a bastard, but he'd taught her one thing. Never let anyone control her. Never again.

Jerking free of Morgan's hand, she knelt to clean up the pieces of broken china, while using the last of the cloths to soak up the spilled water. To hell with the man's headache, he could reuse the cloth he'd been using. He was deliberately tormenting her, keeping her on pins and needles as she waited for him to demand she make good on their wager.

The man seemed to enjoy making her swing in the wind just like Oscar had, waiting until he surprised her with his demand for payment. Surprises were *never* pleasurable. Her husband had taught her they were more often than not, quite painful. Anger and pain rushed through her veins. Damn him. Damn Morgan St. Claire to hell.

Using one of the cloths from the nightstand, she swept it across the floor to wipe up the water. The sudden sharp edge of a broken piece of porcelain she'd missed cut into her finger, and Julia yelped. She climbed to her feet to examine the wound under the light of the candle.

"Let me see."

His harsh command grated on every one of her nerve endings. She wouldn't have cut herself if it hadn't been for his pig-headed behavior. With a shake of her head, she tossed him a disdainful glance over her shoulder before studying the minor cut in the light of the candle.

"I'm fine. It's a small cut."

"Let me see your finger, Julia." The soft words contained a warning note, and she glared at him again before thrusting her hand toward him.

"As I said, it's an insignificant cut."

Morgan studied her finger for a moment then released her hand. His mouth tightened into a firm line as he turned his head away from her. Scowling at him in frustration, she stalked away from his bedside to where she'd dropped her gloves. With quick, jerky movements, she tugged on first one glove and then the other.

Blast the man and his arrogance. The sooner she escaped this den of decadence, the better. It was disturbing enough to know she would return in the future, and not solely of her own volition, but because of her foolish tongue. As she reached the door, he called out to her.

"I shall call on you in two days, Julia."

"I'm afraid I have plans." She threw a glance over her shoulder to see him lying still on the bed, his eyes closed.

"Two days, Julia."

There was no need for Morgan to say anything else. She knew exactly what he meant without any further explanation on his part. If she didn't make herself available to him in two days time, he would extract a price she would not find pleasant. No, that wasn't the problem. The problem was, Julia was worried she might find whatever punishment Morgan St. Claire decided upon would be something she'd enjoy far too much. Not about to answer his autocratic command, she left the room.

Chapter 7

ead bent over her needlepoint, Julia stiffened as the sound of voices in the foyer drifted up the stairs and into the salon. It was easy to distinguish Morgan's voice from that of her butler, Calvert.

A tremor shot through her as she heard heavy footsteps climbing the stairs. What to do? Greet Morgan as though he were expected? No, far better to make it appear that his visit was of little consequence.

Once more, Julia returned her attention to the complex bird of paradise pattern in her hands. She punched the needle through the material just as he entered the parlor. Slowly, she turned her attention toward him in an attempt to illustrate her indifference. There was a smile of amusement on his face, almost as if he could read her mind.

"Good afternoon, Mr. St. Claire. I trust you're feeling better?"

"Exceedingly so."

Glancing back down at her work, she tied off her thread, surprised by the small silence filling the room. Julia darted a look in his direction to find Morgan studying her with narrowed eyes. He looked every inch the gentleman in his dark blue suit coat and a gray vest and trousers. Still, even dressed in the height of fashion, there was a dangerous edge about him. Determined not to lose her composure, she arched an eyebrow as she met his gaze.

"Would you care for a cup of tea? My cook was preparing some scones earlier, I'm certain they're done by now."

"I think a cup of tea would suit me well."

Setting her work on the oval-shaped table next to her wing-backed chair, she rose to her feet. Unnerved by Morgan's presence more than she cared to admit, Julia pressed one hand against the jade silk of her afternoon gown as she moved to ring for tea. The white lace on the sleeve tickled her wrist, reminding her of how he'd stroked her skin the other day. Disturbed by the memory, she tugged on the bell cord a trifle harder than she should have.

A sudden movement flashed just on the edge of her vision, and she jumped slightly before turning to face him. Morgan had moved to stand in front of the brass fire screen, his gaze focused on the small fire burning in the grate. Tension held his jaw line rigid, and Julia tipped her head to one side.

"Is something wrong?" At her question, Morgan's expression immediately changed as he turned to look at her, his smile filled with breathtaking charm.

"Not at all, being in your company is exceptionally pleasant."

"Please save your flattery for someone more susceptible to your charms, St. Claire."

"You seem to enjoy challenging me, Julia. The question is what will you do when I accept?" There was a hint of seduction in his voice that sent a shiver down her back.

"It was not my intent to challenge." She moved toward the center of the room and drew in a sigh of relief at the sight of Calvert entering with a tray of tea and scones. The butler set his burden on the low table in front of the burgundy velvet couch.

"When you rang, Cook thought you would want tea brought up to the salon, madame."

"That was most thoughtful of her. Please thank her for me, Calvert."

The short, stocky servant smiled, then bowed and left the room. To her dismay, he closed the door behind him. Why on earth hadn't she thought to tell him to leave it open? It was bad enough St. Claire was here at all, let alone taking tea with her in such intimate conditions. It might make the servants think the man was courting her. After all, Oscar had been dead for almost two years. It wasn't unheard of for widows to marry again.

Marriage. No. Almost ten years of torment was more than enough for a lifetime. She could still see Oscar sitting in the chair at the fireplace, berating her for speaking to the wrong person at a social gathering. The first time she'd protested, he'd slapped her. The sting of his abuse tingled its way over her skin once more, and she automatically lifted a hand to her cheek. It infuriated him when she would try to explain. She'd learned to tread carefully from that point forward.

Oscar had manipulated her like a puppet at his command. There had been no love or affection. And Julia's worst offense had been her failure to offer him an heir. He'd blamed her for being cold and unresponsive in their bedroom, often punishing her by tying her hands to the bed while he rutted on top of her. Julia flinched at the memory.

She'd fought against believing Oscar's words. Fought desperately. But all the years of mental anguish had taken their toll. Now she was free, and she intended to remain that way. Never again would any man control her as Oscar had.

She closed her eyes for a brief moment to gather her wits before turning back to face her visitor. Morgan smiled at her as he met her gaze. It was a smile filled with devastating charm, and Julia's heart slammed into her chest as the impact of his amused smile affected her senses.

"Your servants are quite efficient," he teased lightly. The sound ignited her senses with awareness. "One would think you'd been expecting company."

"I always have tea at this time of the day—visitors or not." She sent him a cool look before moving to the sofa. Sitting on the edge of the loveseat, she leaned forward and lifted the dainty rose-covered teapot to pour him a cup of tea. As he sat down next to her, the warmth of him engulfed her. With a quick hitch of her breath, she offered him the cup.

It pleased her that her hand remained steady, although inside she was trembling wildly in reaction to his nearness. It was difficult not to be affected by Morgan's overpowering presence and the devastating impact he had on her senses. The size of him was emphasized by the way his hand swallowed the teacup she'd offered him. What would it be like to have his hands cup her, tease her skin. Heavens, what was the matter with her?

Jerking her gaze away from him, she quickly poured herself a cup of tea and took a sip of the scalding beverage. The heat of the tea burned her tongue and she winced with pain. An appropriate punishment for her wicked thoughts. The sudden warmth of Morgan's body sank into hers as he set his cup on the table then leaned into her side.

His spicy male scent flooded Julia's senses as he pulled her cup from her numb fingers. Sweet heaven, why didn't she even offer up a protest? Instead, she was simply allowing him to do as he pleased with her. A hard hand wrapped around the back of her neck, while his thumb pressed into the side of her throat.

"I can always tell when you're nervous or excited. Your pulse flutters wildly, right here." The pad of his thumb caressed the side of her neck in a sensual movement. It teased her skin, causing her heartbeat to increase its pace. "Ah, you see, it skipped again."

"You're imagining things."

"I don't think so, sweetheart." His endearment sent a wave of pleasure through her until she reminded herself that the man was well versed in the seduction of women.

"You are far too full of yourself, St. Claire."

"You called me Morgan the other day." She breathed in the warm smell of sandalwood mixed with spice. It was a fragrant aroma. Heady almost. Her pulse lashed out a frantic beat through her body.

"Did I? I don't recall doing so."

"Perhaps you were too angry with me to remember."

"Only with your stubbornness. I find it quite annoying. In fact, it's the most irritating thing about you."

"So you admit I'm not a hopeless cause after all." There it was again, that teasing note that sent her senses reeling.

"Everyone has a saving grace, even a man such as you."

"Then tell me what my saving graces are, Julia." His mouth caressed her earlobe as he whispered his command into her ear. A shudder rippled through her.

"I cannot....cannot think of them at the moment."

"Not even one?" The warmth of his mouth grazed the point of her jaw line. It shot a volcanic rush of heat through her limbs, leaving behind a languid tranquility in her body.

"No," she breathed. Oh God, she wanted his kiss. She actually craved it. Insane. She had to be insane. It was the only explanation for why she was experiencing these traitorous emotions. The man was a libertine, and she didn't want to be labeled his woman.

"You have a lovely mouth."

His soft words made her gasp. Inside her head, an alarm screamed shrilly for her to take care or she'd be a St. Claire woman in no time at all. No, that wouldn't happen. She'd see to that, but would it hurt to indulge her senses just a little? No man had ever made her want to break all the rules the way this one did.

How it happened, she wasn't certain, but she was no longer sitting upright. Instead, she was reclining back into the couch with a warm body hovering over hers. Dark brown eyes glittered in his handsome face as a smile of satisfaction curled his lips. There was another emotion there as well. It was passion, rich and earthy in its honesty. It struck a chord in her. Excited her.

Every part of her body tingled with sensation as her gaze remained locked with his. God, but he was mesmerizing. Wetting her dry lips, she trembled at the low growl that rumbled in his chest. He lowered his head and grazed her cheek with his mouth. It was a feathery caress, but it made her blood sing with fire.

In the next moment, his mouth tasted hers. It was a light touch, but it stole her breath away. Oblivious to everything else but his kiss, she sighed softly then kissed him back. He immediately pressed his lean, hard body against hers, while her fingers splayed across his chest until she could feel the rhythm of his heartbeat. A lethargic warmth oozed its way into every inch of her body, and she breathed in the delicious heat of his scent.

Her fingers spiked through his hair, the softness of it caressing her skin like silk. He tasted heavenly. Hot and male on her tongue as it danced with his. She'd never realized how a woman's breasts could grow so heavy with desire. The room's cool air brushed across her leg before a warm hand caressed her calf.

Starting with surprise, she murmured a protest. He raised his head, and stared down into her face. If she had been cold, his heated gaze would have been enough to warm her. His hand stroked her leg lightly as he studied her.

"That beautiful mouth can deny it, but your body tells me you're on fire."

The confidence in his voice barely registered as his hand slid up to stroke the skin above her garter. She swallowed hard. This was far more than just an indulgence of her senses. It was a veritable gate to irresistible decadence. She inhaled a sharp breath as his fingers trailed a path over her inner thigh.

"Have you fantasized about me, Julia?"

A fiery heat crested over her cheeks as her gaze darted away from his. While it was true she'd imagined him touching her like this, it had only been in her dreams. She'd not even dared to think of it during the waking hours.

"*No.*"

"Such a charming liar," he said with a disbelieving laugh at her breathless reply. "Well I've had fantasies about you, sweetheart, and in them you're always hot and wet for me."

The wicked words made her look up at him aghast. Speechless, she tried to stop the shiver of anticipation that skimmed over her skin the moment his hand brushed across the apex of her thighs. Her mouth went dry at the dark emotions flashing in his gaze as his finger parted her folds to trace a light circle over the nub hidden inside.

"You're hot and wet now."

The moment his thumb pressed and circled the sensitive area, she shuddered. Excruciating need shot from her belly into the nether regions of her body. Dear Lord, she loved the way he was touching her. A heated rush twisted her insides, and she uttered a small cry as his fingers dipped into her.

"Oh God." She squirmed beneath his heated strokes.

"In your fantasies do I always make you this hot and creamy?" His voice was raw with desire as he teased her with one sensation after another.

She moaned at the explosion of sensation spiraling through her body. Her hips shifted restlessly, writhing beneath his expert touch. Never in her life had she experienced anything like this. Heat engulfed her, and she clutched at his jacket as pleasure streaked through her.

"Admit it, you like what I'm doing to you." His mouth nibbled at her ear.

"N...no. I..."

"Admit *it*." His fingers delved into her in a sinfully delicious thrust and her insides curled with tension.

"Dear Lord, *yes*. Yes, I like it." The words were a hoarse cry of need. In the deep recesses of her mind, she barely recognized the voice as her own. It was as though she was on fire from the inside out. He continued to tease her, his fingers working an incredible magic on her body.

"Soon, quite soon, sweetheart, I'm going to fill you completely. I'm going to enjoy having this tight cunny of yours squeezing on my hot cock until you make me explode with pleasure."

The rough edge to his voice indicated how aroused he was, while the erotic image he'd described only made her hotter, and she bucked against his hand. Her body craved more, and she moaned low in her throat. His thumb swirled around her sensitive nub nestled in her slick folds.

"Damn, you're going to feel good wrapped around my cock. It's going to be like hot, liquid velvet wrapping around me." He rubbed harder at the spot between her legs until the caress tugged the last breath of air from her lungs. With a jerk, her body surged upward against his hand just before she exploded.

Intense waves of sensation rolled over her and small shudders shook her body. Dazed, Julia opened her eyes to look at him. Before she knew what she was doing, her hand cupped his cheek. She could see the desire in his eyes, and she knew he wanted her. And she wanted him. Desperately.

But she couldn't say the words. This was a wager to him. There could only be one night between them. Anything more and she no longer doubted the outcome. She would be well and truly lost. But oh God, how she wanted that night now. This very instant.

As if Morgan could read her mind, he quirked an eyebrow upward and smiled. "No. I don't think so. Not yet, even though the thought is quite tempting."

Appalled by her wanton behavior and the desire still curling in her stomach, Julia shoved her way out of his arms and rose to her feet. She was mortified to know he was toying with her. She didn't want this man to control her, but already his touch was capable of holding her captive to wicked pleasure and delight. The thought frightened and angered her. With shaking hands, she straightened her clothing and tried to regain her composure.

"I think it's time for you to leave, Mr. St. Claire."

"Why? Because I refuse to take you here and now?"

She whirled away and stalked toward the window. Hands pressed against her belly, she tried to still the churning inside her.

"I don't understand you," she said in a voice tight with confusion and fear. "I have said I will honor my debt, and yet you toy with me as a cat does a mouse. I care little for the sensation."

"It's not my intent to toy with you, Julia. But I want you to let go of all your inhibitions, sweetheart. I want the woman I saw in that portrait—lusty, bold and adventurous." Joining her at the window, he turned her to face him. "But most of all, I want you to come to my bed of your own free will."

"That portrait was not for anyone to see. It's not real. That woman doesn't exist." Fists clenching the fabric of her green silk skirts, she grew stiff as a metal rod as he dipped his head toward her.

"You're wrong, Julia. That woman exists. A talented artist always sees beneath the surface. You're simply afraid."

"I am not," she exclaimed with anger. But even as she spoke, she knew he was right. And she hated being forced to admit Morgan St. Claire might be right about something where she was concerned. She watched his eyes narrow with a speculative gleam until determination filled his expression.

One hand pressed against the base of her throat, Julia inhaled a ragged breath. God help her, she didn't know how she was going to fulfill her wager without losing a part of herself to him. He studied her for a long moment before he shook his head with a gleam of frustration in his dark brown eyes.

"Today was a step in the right direction. We'll see about expanding your horizons tomorrow night at the St. Claire Fete."

His soft voice sent trepidation sliding down her back. No. She needed to throw herself on his mercy and have done with it. If he continued this seduction, she would be lost. Not looking at him, she laced her fingers together, trying not to tremble.

"Wouldn't tonight be a better opportunity?" The sooner this was done, the sooner she could regain her sanity.

"No, I have an appointment this evening."

For a fleeting instant, she found herself wondering what woman would be in his bed tonight. It wouldn't be her, and the knowledge nipped at her like an angry puppy. She turned away from him to watch the traffic in the street below. The sinewy arm suddenly wrapped around her waist made her gasp as he pulled her back into his chest. His mouth nibbled at her ear.

"And no, my sweet beauty, it's not another woman."

Appalled that he'd been able to read her thoughts, she jerked away from him and put several feet between them. "I care little as to whom you entertain, St. Claire."

"So you say—but your face is quite expressive, Julia. Even more so when you climax beneath my touch."

With a wicked grin on his lips, Morgan strode from the salon, leaving her to sputter with indignation as the door closed behind him. The man was insufferable and far too arrogant. Climax indeed. The thought made her cheeks burn with mortification. When a woman had sexual relations with her husband or lover, it was supposed to be about the man's pleasure. Oscar had made that very clear.

The memory chilled her. Pleasure had been the farthest thing from her husband's mind when he'd come to her bed.

He'd been a rutting boar, spilling his seed in her without one thought of her comfort or pleasure.

Her husband had disgusted her. She'd been grateful when after nearly two years of marriage he'd stopped coming to her bed. Her inability to have a child had earned her nothing but his contempt, but she had gladly accepted it in place of his sexual attentions.

A tremor wracked her body as she remembered how differently Morgan made her feel. She had experienced no disgust at his touch. In truth, it had been exciting. Exhilarating even. The thought made Julia's heart skip. She did not want to let the man excite or exhilarate her. She simply wanted to fulfill her debt and be done with him.

Of course, what she wanted and what Morgan St. Claire wanted were two different things. The man wouldn't disappear from her life until it suited him. And *that* was what worried her.

Chapter 8

Standing in the loft overlooking the warehouse floor, Morgan watched the spirited party below. The building had been emptied for the annual St. Claire Fete, and at one end of the large storage facility, the small orchestra he'd hired was playing an Irish jig. On the makeshift dance floor, his employees and their guests danced with an exuberance that pleased him. There was unrestrained freedom in the boisterous antics of the dancers as they cavorted to the music.

Like the partygoers, Morgan wore no jacket, and the sleeves of his shirt were rolled up past his elbows. He wanted his employees to feel comfortable. Dressing in the same manner they did removed the barrier of wealth that usually existed between them. His father was no doubt rolling in his grave. The man had always worked his employees hard, never realizing that people were inclined to work harder when they were treated well.

When his father had died, Morgan had made changes almost overnight. His actions had propelled St. Claire Shipping even further out in front of its competitors until it was even more successful now than it had been in his father's time. A grim smile of satisfaction tilted one corner of his mouth. It would have irritated his father immensely to know that his son had proven to be a better business man.

Morgan's shoe tapped lightly against the planks of the loft floor as his gaze scanned the activities below. Across the dance floor from the band, temporary tables made out of sawhorses and planks lined the wall. Covered with colorful blue-checked tablecloths, the tables sagged with a bountiful assortment of meats, vegetables, breads and the Clarendon's famous cranberry scones.

It was a sight never seen in his father's time, but then his father had never been one to coddle the workers. His father had thought solely of his own amusement. Morgan clenched his jaw as he remembered the lack of interest his father had shown in him until he came of age. Then the man had wanted him to take on the family business. Originally, Morgan had thought to refuse, but short of funds, he'd had little choice.

When his father had died only a few months after Morgan joined the company, he'd had the opportunity to rid himself of St. Claire Shipping. Something inside him compelled him not to sell, and the decision to keep the business had made him a wealthy man. For all intents and purposes, Morgan was content with his life, but occasionally he felt as though something were missing.

He frowned as the word *home* whispered its way through his head. Morgan immediately scoffed at the notion. The idea that he needed a place to call home was laughable. The Clarendon was all that he needed in the way of a home. A miserable childhood with an indifferent father and a mother who found the sight of him unbearable was enough to convince even the hardiest of souls not to wish for a place to call home. Morgan's jaw tightened at the unpleasant memories.

On the floor below, he saw an older couple enjoying the party from the sidelines. The man had an arm around his wife as he spoke into her ear. It amazed Morgan how many of his employees were happily married despite their harsh lives. On occasion, he'd visited their homes to check on sick employees. Despite their woes, there was a warmth in their homes that he'd envied until he reminded himself of his childhood.

As a boy, Morgan had believed a home of his own would be someplace he could escape to, but when he was old enough, he realized it wasn't possible. A house symbolized marriage and all the discord that went with it. And marriage was an institution to be avoided at any cost. Shrugging off the morose images of the past, he folded his arms across his chest and studied the party goers below.

From this height, Morgan could easily see the comings and goings of everyone in the building. Several of his investors stood around the large keg of ale he'd brought in for the occasion. His most important investor had yet to arrive, and Morgan shrugged his shoulders in an impatient gesture. He didn't like the fact that he was so eager to see Julia.

The woman was occupying his thoughts far too much for his comfort. He simply needed to bed her and get his lust for her out of his system. The moment the thought filled his head, Morgan knew that wasn't possible. If he claimed his winnings before he'd wooed Julia sufficiently, the end result wouldn't be to his liking. He wanted more than one night with Julia in his bed, and fulfilling the wager now would ensure he only had one night with her.

He needed to take his time with her. Julia was a complex creature, but he was certain of one thing. Fear kept her wrapped up in that mantle of repression she wore with such vigor. But she'd not been able to completely suppress her curiosity. It was there in her eyes, in the way she responded to his kisses. Even more intriguing was that she didn't seem to fear society's judgment. If that were true, she never would have dared to invest her money in St. Claire Shipping or any other business venture.

Not to mention her active involvement with her investment. No, Julia wasn't frightened by society's opinion. If anything, she demonstrated her determination to flaunt the restrictive rules of present day mores. No, something else frightened her. The key to unlocking Julia so she became the woman in Peebles's painting was discovering out what really frightened her.

Out of the corner of his eye, Morgan saw one of his younger clerks bow to a partner before sweeping her into his arms and out onto the floor. Again, his gaze swept over the crowd below him searching for some sign of Julia. Damn it, where was she? The muscle in his jaw tightened at the thought she might not have any intention of coming despite her words to the contrary. His fingers bit into his arms as he glared down at the dancers. Christ Jesus, one would think he'd lost his senses when it came to the woman.

Morgan caught another glimpse of his clerk spinning his partner around the dance floor and frowned. There was something familiar about the woman's dark hair. The way the light caught the golden highlights in the dark red— damnation. With a grunt of exasperation, he wheeled on the back of his heel and strode along the loft's landing to the stairs leading to the floor.

She'd lost her mind. It was the only explanation. Why else would she dress like one of his employees and dance with Bentley? The woman obviously didn't realize how easily her presence could stir up trouble with men who'd been drinking. Not to mention the potential for jealousy where the womenfolk were concerned. The music came to a halt as he reached the dance floor.

Weaving his way through the crowd, he saw the clerk bow once more in front of Julia. Flushed from the exertion of the dance, she was radiant. Hell, she wasn't just radiant— she looked exactly like Peebles had painted her. His groin immediately tightened. Julia was laughing at something the boy had said when he came to a halt in front of them.

From the way Bentley blanched as their eyes met, Morgan knew his expression was forbidding. Damnation, the boy didn't deserve his anger. The only person deserving of his ire was himself. From the beginning, Julia had twisted him into knots, and his fascination hadn't abated. If anything, it was growing in a way that made him feel possessive of her. Determined to put his clerk at ease, Morgan forced a smile to his lips. "I see you managed to persuade Mrs. Westgard to take to the floor, Bentley."

"Yes…yes, sir, Mr. St. Claire. I didn't like seeing her standing on the sidelines. Wasn't socially polite."

The firm resolve in Bentley's voice made Morgan's smile widen. The lad would go far in the company. It wasn't often one of his employees had the gumption to politely tell Morgan to go hang himself.

"I like a man who does the right thing, Bentley. Now off you go to get something to drink. I'll see to Mrs. Westgard." Jerking his head in the direction of the keg of ale, he sent the clerk on his way.

As the young man disappeared from view, the orchestra launched into a new song. Without asking her permission, he pulled Julia into his arms. Her gasp of surprise made her mouth form a soft moue, and Morgan grinned as he whirled her about in several quick turns. She wasn't wearing gloves, and he liked the way her fingers clung to his arms.

He half expected her to protest angrily, but she didn't. Instead, she tipped her head back and smiled. Morgan inhaled a sharp breath. When she smiled like that, he was close to offering her the world. Somewhere an alarm went off in his head, but he crushed it into silence. Whirling her around in another small circle, he dipped his head toward her.

"Perhaps you would care to explain your manner of dress for this evening."

"My dress?" She frowned in puzzlement before understanding cleared her furrowed brow. "Oh—you mean my borrowed clothing. I didn't want the women comparing their own dresses to anything I wore. No one should ever be made to feel inadequate. It's not a pleasant experience."

Stunned, Morgan stared down at her in amazement. No other woman of his acquaintance would have ever thought of doing such a thing. For some reason, her actions pleased him enormously. His arms tightened around her as he pressed his body into hers. She was warm and soft against him.

"You say that as if someone has made you feel inadequate at one time or another." He watched her eyes darken with a pain that made him want to comfort her.

"My late husband made it a habit to point out my numerous faults."

"Numerous?" He chuckled. "I find it hard to believe he could have found that much to find fault with, Julia."

"Oscar took exception to a great many things," she said with a quiet bitterness that surprised him.

"Would he have taken exception to your attending tonight's event?"

"Most assuredly," she said. There was a pronounced echo of satisfaction in her voice as she smiled tightly. "Oscar would have been appalled by my investing his money in St. Claire Shipping, and he would have…been horrified that I was here among the common folk."

Something about the way she stumbled over her words told Morgan she had been about to say something entirely different. Once again, she aroused a protective instinct in him. How Westgard could have found anything to disapprove of when it came to Julia, puzzled him.

She wasn't just beautiful. Her actions showed a compassionate heart. Helping the poor was a cause many of the wealthy took up. But something told him the orphanage was more important to Julia than it was to others of her social status. Even her manner of dress this evening illustrated her consideration for the feelings of others.

The fact that she'd dressed specifically to avoid making his employees uncomfortable didn't just impress him. It made him like her. He'd never met any woman quite like her. As Morgan swung her around the dance floor, he smiled at the look of pleasure on Julia's face.

"You enjoy dancing." His observation didn't require her response, but her smile made his heart race like a steam engine pounding its way down a railroad track.

"Very much, unless of course my feet are being trampled by a terrible partner," she said with a laugh, the haunted look in her eyes gone.

"And do you find me a poor partner?"

"Not at all," she said with a small laugh. "You're an excellent dancer."

"So you like being in my arms then." Morgan flashed her a wicked grin, enjoying the blush that rose in her lovely face.

"Somehow I think you mean something entirely different."

"You know *exactly* what I mean," he said with soft deliberation.

The thought of holding her naked in his arms made his muscles tighten. Their eyes met, and he saw the tip of her pink tongue flick out to wet her lips. His mouth went dry at the effect such a small action had on him.

"You're an extraordinary woman, Julia."

"You've been in the ale already." She averted her gaze, her voice stiff and cool. "There's nothing special about me at all."

"Ah, but you're wrong. I've seen the woman beneath that shroud of repressed emotions you wear."

"I don't know *what* you mean."

"You're a terrible liar, Julia. You know exactly what I'm talking about. I just want to know why you enjoy hiding behind this cool façade."

"I'm not hiding from anything," she snapped. "I am being circumspect."

For a moment, he just stared down at her in astonishment before he laughed out loud. With a shake of his head, he laughed again at her irate expression. "Do you call your portrait circumspect? And I'd hardly call the theft of my handkerchief a discreet adventure, would you?"

"I told you why I took the handkerchief."

"Yes, but I'm not convinced you stole my handkerchief simply to raise funds for that orphanage of yours."

He pulled her closer and deftly whirled her out of the path of an overly exuberant couple on the dance floor. The swell of her breast pressed into his arm, and he realized how much it pleased him to have her in his arms. It felt right. Morgan wasn't sure how he knew that. He simply knew he'd never felt this way before when holding a woman.

"What other possible reason could I have for stealing your handkerchief?"

"I don't know. Perhaps you enjoyed the excitement of doing something a *respectable* husband might disapprove of." Her eyes widened with surprise, and she recovered quickly, but not before he knew he'd hit a nerve.

"You're mistaken. And if I hadn't been caught red-handed by you, we wouldn't be having this conversation at all." Her haughty tone challenged him.

"If you truly believe that, then you're the one who's mistaken," he said quietly. "And perhaps it's time I showed you why."

"Good lord. Tonight?" Her cool demeanor gone, she met his gaze with an anxious look.

Damnation, she looked as though she thought he would eat her. The thought of doing just that was a fleeting one, and Morgan released a quiet breath of frustration. The woman was a conundrum. He should abandon the wager entirely, but something inside him refused to let her go. The woman tempted him in ways he'd yet to understand. It wasn't just an unexpected feeling. It was an unfamiliar one. It signified something, and Morgan wasn't sure if it was good or bad.

With the last note of the music drifting through the air, he swung her off the dance floor. Uncertainty swept across

Julia's features as the color drained from her face. With a quick move, she left his arms. Morgan could have held onto her, but he let her go without any objection. Hazel eyes wide in her oval face, she stared up at him with apprehension, but a hint of excitement shimmered in her gaze too.

In silence, he studied her for a long moment before making up his mind. Whatever fear kept her enshrined in that cloak of virtue, Morgan intended to strip it away. That tiny glimmer of anticipation in Julia's gaze was all the invitation he needed. He might not bed her tonight, but he was damn well going to give her a taste of what to expect. Igniting her desire might even take the painful edge off his lust. Besides, the thought of hearing her plead for more was a pleasurable one.

Music swelled around them again as he caught her by the arm and guided her toward the warehouse door. With little effort, he guided her out into the night with only one or two employees taking notice. Everyone else was too busy enjoying the party to concern themselves with the actions of their employer. The crisp spring air nipped at his skin as Julia suddenly regained her voice.

"What do you think you're doing, St. Claire?"

"Taking you to a place where we'll not be interrupted." He tightened his grip on her as she almost managed to slip away from him.

Crossing the street, he reached awkwardly into his vest pocket for his office key. The cool metal warmed in his hand as they stopped in front of his shipping offices. When Morgan pushed the door leading into the main office open, he gently, but firmly, forced her through it. Julia immediately uttered a sound of protest.

"We should return to the party. Everyone is going to notice that we've left."

"Let them," Morgan growled as he closed and locked the door behind them.

Moonlight drifted through the glass windows of the main office, which lit their way to the door that opened up into his personal domain. The door of his office gave way with a loud screech, and Morgan remembered he needed to have someone oil the hinges. Inside the spacious room, he ushered her to the chair in front of his desk.

"Sit, and don't move."

When Julia balked at his rough command, he forced her to sink down into the leather chair. She huffed with outraged annoyance, but Morgan didn't respond. In quick succession, he locked the office door, drew the window shades and turned up the gas light sconce on the wall. The moment he turned around, Morgan saw Julia had risen from the chair he'd ordered her to sit in. Chin tilted at a defiant angle, she stood in front of his desk, her demeanor that of a prim and proper governess.

"I do not appreciate your high-handed behavior St. Claire, and I have a distinct dislike for surprises of any kind." Julia's voice was sharp with irritation, but Morgan ignored her dissension.

"Unbutton your dress, Julia." At his command, her jaw sagged, and she stared at him in stunned disbelief.

"I beg your pardon?"

"The buttons on your shirtwaist, Julia. Undo them." In the blink of an eye, her appalled expression changed to belligerent anger. Julia shook her head vehemently.

"I will do no such thing," she snapped. "If you have suddenly decided to collect my—"

"Would you prefer I do it for you, instead?"

Morgan arched an arrogant eyebrow as he cooly met Julia's rebellious gaze. Arms folded across his chest, he waited patiently for her to comply with his command. The moment she accepted the fact he wasn't about to give way in his demand, she expelled a breath of disgusted anger. In an abrupt movement, her fingers quickly undid the buttons running from the base of her throat down to her waist.

Fury glittered in her hazel eyes as she glared at him and silently dared him to do his worst. She was beautiful and radiant in her anger. God help him when this woman came apart in his arms. Morgan's groin tightened at the image forming in his head, and he slowly closed the space between them.

There was only a hint of trepidation in Julia's gaze as he approached her, and she gamely stood her ground. Although she'd undone the buttons of her dress, Julia hadn't pulled the garment open, so he could only see a small portion of her corset. It didn't matter, the only reason he'd made her unbutton her shirtwaist was to keep her from using her clothing as an emotional shield against what he planned. With less than a foot separating them, Morgan reached out and trailed his finger from the side of her neck to the base of her throat.

The instant she trembled at his touch, a hot blast of desire surged through him, swelling his cock until he was hard with need. Damnation, never in all his life had he ever wanted a woman as much as he wanted Julia. He wanted to take her hard and fast, then, after they'd had time to recover, he wanted to take his time exploring every delectable inch of her.

"I've never known a woman whose skin was as soft as yours. It's like silk against my fingers."

"What game are you playing, St. Claire? This is not part of the wager. You said one night in your bed." There was a breathless quality to her voice, and it shot an arrow of excitement through him.

"The wager was that I wanted the woman in the portrait in my bed. And I'll do whatever it takes to pull her out from underneath that prim and proper façade you insist on hiding behind."

"I've told you before, the woman you saw doesn't exist. She's a figment of Peebles's imagination."

Not answering her, Morgan removed his vest, then slowly unbuttoned his shirt. Julia's eyes widened as she watched him with stunned fascination. The tip of her pink tongue flicked out to wet her lips, and the enticing sight made him ache to have her mouth wrapped around his cock. Lust fired his blood at the thought, but his goal at the moment was to break through Julia's cool reserve.

If he wanted the woman in the portrait in his bed, he needed to show Julia how to be completely uninhibited where he was concerned. When his fingers had undone the last button of his shirt, he tugged the garment free of his trousers. Eager to feel her touch, Morgan shrugged off his shirt then tossed it over the back of the chair facing his desk.

"I want you to touch me."

"*Touch* you?" Julia's eyes widened with surprise, but he saw excitement flit across her lovely face before she tightened her mouth into a thin, prudish line.

"Yes. Touch me."

"I most certainly will not," she exclaimed. The moment she tried to slip past him, Morgan blocked her escape. Drawing in a harsh breath, he caught her hand and pressed it into his chest.

Her palm was hot against his skin, and his body tensed with need. Christ Jesus, even when he had to coerce her to touch him, he was ready to spill his seed. Bewilderment darkened her face as Julia stared up at him.

"Why can't you simply take your winnings, then leave me be?" The whispered plea held the unmistakable note of fear. Something twisted inside him the instant the answer to her question tried to push its way out of the depths of his mind. It set off alarms in his head, but he willed the answer into oblivion.

"Stop talking, and just touch me," he growled as he struggled to keep from tugging her into his arms and kissing her into submission.

Chapter 9

Julia stared at her hand pressed into the hard masculine chest in front of her. Once more, it was impossible not to marvel at how beautiful his body was. Julia jumped as Morgan caught her other hand and pressed it into his bare flesh. Unprepared for his almost passive assault on her senses, she shuddered as the warm flesh beneath her palms stirred a wild sensation inside her.

Desire, excitement, anticipation, and fear slid sluggishly through Julia's veins. The conflicting emotions made her tremble as he gently encouraged her hands to explore him. Beneath her fingertips, Morgan was hot, flexible steel as she traced the hard lines and planes of his muscular chest.

Everywhere her fingers went, the warmth of him sank through her pores and into her blood. She found herself torn between leisurely exploring his body and the need to beg for his kisses. Only in her innermost thoughts had she wondered what it would be like to touch him like this.

Not even yesterday afternoon when Morgan's intimate caresses had set her on fire had she experienced such an intense craving for a man's touch. His touch. Desire flooded her senses and lodged an ache inside her. All she wanted was for there to be nothing but skin between them as she allowed him to conquer her body and mind. Her soul she refused to give up, but God how she wanted him at this moment.

She swallowed hard, struggling to fight the hunger unfurling inside her belly. As she explored him, her fingers glided over the thin line of hair that trailed its way from the middle of his chest downward until it disappeared into his trousers.

Just touching him was a heady experience, but it was the unexpected sight of his arousal beneath his trousers that made her inhale a sharp breath. Between her thighs, her sex tightened with a pleasurable ache as she took in the thick size of him. She jerked her head up to see the dark passion burning in his eyes. As their gazes met, her fingers against his body conveyed to her the precise second his breathing changed from a steady rhythm to one that was ragged and heavy with restrained passion.

What was holding him back from devouring her? Why didn't he kiss her—caress her until she was sobbing for him to complete her. The craving that had been building inside her made her head swim with wicked thoughts and sinful images. If he had thought to bring her to her knees until she willingly surrendered to him, he'd won.

All he had to do was make a demand, and she wouldn't hesitate to do whatever he asked of her. He leaned into her until his mouth was just a hair's breadth from hers. The faintest scent of whiskey feathered its way past her nostrils. It blended with his scent to tantalize her senses as she realized how badly she wanted to lose her self-control with this man.

Without thinking, she leaned into him and pressed her mouth against his. The whiskey on his breath made him taste hot and spicy. For a brief moment, his lips welcomed hers. A second later, his head snapped up, and he sucked in a sharp breath, his jaw rigid with tension. Strong hands bit into her waist and he lifted her off her feet to set her down on top of his desk.

Startled, she stared up at him in bewilderment. The dangerous glint in his blue eyes sent a shiver of delicious expectation across her skin. It spiraled through her blood and sank deeper until it reached the heart of her.

"Please, Morgan…" she whispered.

"Now, I'm going to prove to you why I know the lady in the portrait is real," he rasped darkly.

His mouth captured hers again in a hard, demanding kiss. It assailed every one of her senses and became a fiery storm that threatened to consume her as his tongue swept into her mouth. In the pit of her belly, the sensations he'd stirred to life in her yesterday returned to engulf her.

Inside the stiff leather of her corset, her breasts swelled and tightened, while her nipples hardened into stiff peaks. Nerve endings cried out a sharp protest to the silk of her chemise scraping across the hard tips of her breasts. Wicked and sinful, her sensitive flesh hovered between exquisite pain and pleasure from the sensations assaulting her. Sweet heaven, she wanted to feel his hands on her again. She wanted, no needed, to have him touching her the way he had yesterday.

As if reading her mind, Morgan dragged her skirts upward until the material was gathered together in her lap. In the next beat of her heart, the hot steel of his palm cupped one side of her buttocks and lifted her up just enough to roughly tug her drawers downward and off her legs. Startled, she gasped before a delicious anticipation swept through her.

Cool air brushed across her thighs as Morgan nudge her legs apart and planted himself between them, then leaned into her. Hard and powerful, his body pressed into hers and forced her backward until she was lying on the desk. She knew she should be shocked by his actions, but it was impossible to think straight as she lost herself in the hot pleasure of his kiss.

When his mouth suddenly left hers, she murmured a protest and watched him straighten upright. She made to follow him, but a large hand pressed her back onto the desk. Blue eyes blazing with desire, the wicked smile curving his sensual mouth made her ache with longing for him to continue kissing her.

"No. Stay where you are."

Confused, she obeyed him then gasped as a large, warm hand ran up along her inner thigh. When his fingers found the outer rim of her sex, she jumped at the light caress. A low chuckle escaped him, and he stroked her again.

"You like that, don't you, my sweet beauty?"

She could only respond with a whimper of need at the teasing caress before she gasped in surprise as he suddenly took a step back and spread her legs wide. Completely exposed to him, her face burned as if on fire as she saw the way he stood spell-bound staring down at the apex of her thighs.

"My, God," he exclaimed hoarsely. "You have the loveliest cunny I've ever seen, sweetheart. If Peebles had painted these lush pink folds of yours, glistening with heat, I would have to kill him simply for having seen you this way. Even my cock is in awe of your beauty, and its demanding I fuck you right here and now."

Lust had reduced Morgan's voice to a primal growl, which made his profane words sound even darker. She was well-acquainted with profanities, but her husband's use of them had only disgusted her. When they'd rolled off Morgan's tongue, she'd experienced no revulsion or disgust. If anything, they simply intensified her desire and craving for him. Slowly, he lifted his gaze to meet hers, and the passionate hunger in his piercing blue gaze sent her heartbeat skidding out of control.

"Yesterday, I asked if you'd had any fantasies about me," he said softly, as his gaze shifted downward again. "I don't think I mentioned all the fantasies I've had of you."

Her gasp became a low moan as his fingers stroked the edge of her core briefly. Unable to suppress her reaction, a tremor rippled through her, while her sex ached for more of his touch. The sensation became a blistering wave of heat as he slid two fingers into her. The intimate caress pulled another moan from her.

God, she wanted him to pleasure her the same way he had yesterday. She wanted to feel that delicious pressure building inside her until she shattered into a million pieces. Their gazes met, and the wicked smile curving his sensual mouth made her draw in a sharp breath of anticipation.

"Shall I tell you about one of my fantasies, sweetheart?"

Sinful and seductive, his voice ignited an unquenchable thirst for his touch as his hand pulled away from her. She licked her dry lips, about to plead with him not to stop. But he stole her breath away the instant his smile dissolved into an expression of sin at its most basic of levels. Morgan's voice grew hoarse as his gaze remained locked with hers.

"In my fantasy, I dip my tongue into your hot cream. I lick every bit of it off your soft, velvety pink folds."

For the first time, Morgan shocked her. Surely he didn't mean to do what she thought he was suggesting. Julia's eyes widened, and she quickly tried to slide away from him. A slow smile tilted his lips upward as his strong hands held her firmly in place.

"No, my sweet beauty, there's nowhere to run," he murmured with a soft chuckle. "I've wanted to taste you since the day you entered this office with your solicitor, and if you think I'm willing to wait any longer, you're mistaken."

"Dear God, you can't possibly mean—"

"Oh, but I do, sweetheart. I'm going to fuck you with my tongue."

Husky and low, his wicked words tugged a low moan from her as every muscle in her sex tighten. Held immobile by his strength, she watched in dismay as Morgan sank to his knees and lowered his head toward the apex of her thighs. Fire erupted inside her as his tongue swirled around the rim of her sex.

Cast into a whirlpool of pleasure, a wild cry of ecstasy flowed out of her. Her orgasm was almost instantaneous, and her body jerked hard against his sinful mouth and the hot strokes of his tongue. The wickedness of it was hedonistic, enthralling, and the most wonderful thing she'd ever experienced.

"Christ Jesus, you taste good." His voice was husky with passion as he nibbled at the inside of her thigh. "You're dripping with hot honey."

His tongue swept across her slick folds once more sending flames speeding over her skin in a blinding cascade of delicious sensation. Fingers digging into his hard shoulders, another keening cry of pleasure escaped her as his tongue stroked its way along her inner folds. Just when she didn't think her pleasure could be outmatched, his teeth scraped across the sensitive spot inside her folds.

She barely had time to breathe before his lips clamped down on the tender nub of flesh. It made her buck hard against his mouth as she released a cry of gratification. Gently, his mouth and teeth nibbled and tugged on her flesh, and she was reduced to a state of delirious rapture.

With each wild, sinful sensation that clutched at her sex, she experienced a longing for something she couldn't put into words. Was this what sex was really suppose to be like? It was unlike anything she'd even dared to dream. She felt as if she were a star about to explode from the intense reaction at its core. Pressure suddenly rose and unfurled inside her before it etched its way down to where he was tending to her so intimately.

She shuddered as he continued to pleasure her. Never had she experienced anything so erotic or exhilarating. The man controlled her every thought and reaction, but she didn't care. If giving up control meant experiencing this kind of passion, it was worth the price of making herself vulnerable. Her body was his to command.

"Oh dear God," she panted in rapid breaths as the pressure building inside her reached a fervent pitch. "*Morgan.*"

She screamed his name then exploded in a splinter of tiny shards of sinful delight. Mindlessly, she shattered beneath his hedonistic caresses, her body arching upward as another keening cry of blissful exaltation flew past her lips.

The aftermath of her climax left Julia trembling as she lay spent on Morgan's desk, unable to move. Eyes closed, she felt the male heat of him rise and hover over her. Gently nibbling at the side of her neck, his teeth grazed her earlobe.

"You enjoyed yourself," he whispered in her ear.

It wasn't a question, and all she could do was make an incoherent sound of agreement. Oblivious to anything but the lethargic heat coating her body, it took her several seconds to realized Morgan had picked her up in his arms. Cradled against him, Julia sighed softly as he sank down into one of the chairs to hold her in his lap. Strong muscular arms held her close, and his embrace invoked a feeling of being protected from harm.

Through her clothing, Morgan's hard length pressed against her thigh. Startled, she realized he was still aroused, and yet his only thought seemed centered around her pleasure. The knowledge stunned her. Not once had Oscar *ever* shown her such consideration. That Morgan would sacrifice his own pleasure simply to ensure hers aroused unexpected emotions inside Julia.

If the man continued to seduce her so patiently, there would be no hope of resisting him. The man already held too much sway over her. With a glance up into his eyes, she grew stiff with tension. Satisfaction glittered in his gaze. He believed he had won. Well, hadn't he?

For all intents and purposes, she was a St. Claire woman. He'd branded her in the most intimate way possible. The thought cleared her head as she acknowledged the truth. No matter how skillfully he'd pleasured her, their association was becoming far too dangerous.

She could not allow it to continue. Never again would she submit to any man's control. Once had been enough, and where Morgan St. Claire was concerned, control was everything. He lived and breathed control. Even their wager had been an issue of control for him.

He'd seen to it she would lose, and ensured his victory. Any prolonged involvement with him meant Julia would be at his disposal until he chose to cast her aside with only a handkerchief as a memento of their association. Glancing away from him, she tensed as a warm finger stroked the side of her neck.

"Next time, I intend to come inside you, sweetheart, and I promise you'll melt."

Morgan's words ignited fear inside her. What was she going to do? She had to keep him at bay somehow. He'd already demolished her physical resistance. If she didn't take care, it would be her heart next. Clarity struck at that precise moment.

He'd said he wanted her in his bed willingly. If she went to him of her own volition, then she would be free. They would have one blissful night, and then he could make no further demands of her. It was the only way she could protect herself. The longer she put off the payment of the wager, the more tenuous her position when it came to escaping with her heart intact.

"Morgan." When she spoke his name, he nuzzled the side of her neck.

"Hmm."

"I…I would like…would you take me to your rooms tonight."

She tensed as he grew still and silent against her. There was something disturbing about his tautness that increased her tension. Fearful that he might have found her request insincere, she trailed her forefinger down the middle of his chest until her fingers rested at the top of his trousers.

Confidence swelled inside her when she heard him suck in a harsh breath. The sound gave her the courage to slide one finger between him and the material of the waistband. She was about to reach for the buttons holding his fly closed when Morgan's large hand covered hers.

Meeting his gaze, she saw a hunger in his eyes that was as hypnotic as it was alarming.

Was it already too late? Had she already crossed the point where no matter how far she might run, he would always be in her thoughts? Yet, even as frightening as that question was, the dark passion glittering in his blue eyes excited her. With the same lazy power of a jungle cat, Morgan abruptly set her on her feet and rose to tower over her.

"No. Not tonight." He shook his head as he cupped her face and kissed her gently. "I said willingly, Julia. At the moment, your body wants me, but I'm not so sure your head does. If you still feel the same way tomorrow night, then come to me. I want no regrets."

She flinched at his words. There would always be regrets. He wanted her in his bed emotionally as well as physically—unfettered by the past. But that wasn't something she could do. When she went to him, it would be for one glorious night and nothing more. There was no other way. With a nod of her head, she moved away from him.

Aware of how disheveled her appearance must be, she quickly buttoned up the front of her shirtwaist. Out of the corner of her eyes, she saw Morgan shove a hand through his hair in what she thought might have been frustration.

Was he regretting his refusal to bed her tonight? There was a fierce expression of concentration on his handsome features. Watching him surreptitiously, Julia barely managed to stave off a quick inhalation of pleasure as his wide shoulders flexed, and he shrugged his shirt on. He truly was magnificent.

A lock of hair dangled against her cheek, and Julia turned her attention to making herself look presentable. She didn't want to return to the party, but she preferred to look respectable if someone were to cross her path. Quickly rearranging her hair, she turned toward Morgan when she'd repaired her appearance as best as she possibly could.

There was a dark frown on his beautiful, masculine features, and as he finished tucking his shirt into his pants, he stared down at the floor. When he didn't say anything, Julia took a step toward him.

"Morgan?"

His head snapped up to look at her, and she saw his mouth tighten with determination. In three quick strides, he crossed the floor to stand in front of her. Alarmed, Julia trembled slightly, but didn't retreat. Instead, she met his gaze unwaveringly. His hands cupped her face, and he kissed her with restrained passion. Lifting his head, his eyes met hers and she shivered. It was as if he could see into her soul, and the thought terrified her.

"Tonight I broke through that icy shell of yours, Julia. Tomorrow night I intend to see that shell shattered completely." The confidence in his voice made her stomach lurched, but she fought back her fear and smiled.

"And I shall see if the great St. Claire's reputation is all it is said to be."

The irreverent words caught him by surprise, and his jaw sagged. She laughed with genuine amusement and more than a hint of triumph. With a grin, he tugged her into his arms.

"I promise you, sweetheart," he growled. "Tomorrow night you won't think about anything else *except* my wicked reputation as I intend to pleasure you until dawn."

Morgan didn't give her a chance to respond as he captured her mouth again and proceeded to give her a taste of what she had to look forward too.

Chapter 10

The sweet smell of new grass teased her senses as Julia trotted along the riding track in Hyde Park. It was early yet. Far too early for fashionable members of the Set to be out riding or walking in the park. She'd not slept well and instead of continuing to toss in her bed, she'd decided to go for a ride.

Usually the fresh air was enough to clear her head so she could think straight. But that wasn't the case today. If anything, her thoughts were all the more cloudy than when she'd still been in bed. Tonight she would go to Morgan as she'd agreed, but she wondered if he would deduce her intention never to share his bed again once tomorrow morning arrived. Something about him said he would want to continue their affair. *That*, she wasn't prepared to do.

There was no doubt the man was a skilled lover. Fire skimmed the surface of her skin every time he was near. He was a master at making her feel things no man ever had. With each touch, she wanted to melt into his arms and forget everything except the fact that he was making love to her.

Now, in the light of day, her decision was not as clear-cut as she'd thought. The heated passion of the night had given way to the cold shadows of the morning. And fear was the primary shadow. Fear of giving herself over to his complete control.

But even more frightening was the fact she was more than willing to give up control simply to experience heaven in his arms. The traitorous thought made Julia heave a sigh. There was no other option available to her. Tonight she would go to Morgan's bed willingly. And there would be no doubt in his mind, *or hers*, that it was of her own volition. But would she have the strength to leave him when morning came?

With a nudge of her heel, she urged Solomon into a canter. A short time later she reached the end of the narrow track and turned about to return in the direction she'd come. As she did so, she caught sight of Morgan riding toward her.

He cut a fine figure on his gray mount—so fine that he stole her breath away. She tried to check the desire that abruptly soared through her. But the moment she did so, a small voice reminded her that there was no reason she couldn't enjoy the time she had left in Morgan's company.

After tonight, they would go their separate ways, and his touch would only be a memory. She would allow herself to savor the pleasure of his company, if even for just these few short hours. Her mouth went dry as he pulled alongside of her, a wickedly charming smile on his sensual lips.

"Good morning, Julia."

"St. Claire." She nodded her head in greeting as he reined in his animal to walk beside hers.

"I think we're beyond such formality, don't you? Especially given the fact that I can still taste you on my tongue."

The audacious words made her gasp as she glared at him. "How can you mention something so…so…hedonistic in the light of day?"

"If I sound epicurean, so be it." He shrugged. "But I confess that the taste of your delicious hot honey on my tongue has pleased me more than anything in recent memory."

Unable to respond, she stared at him in shock while the heat of embarrassment burned her cheeks . His obvious amusement only enhanced his good looks, and he grinned with almost boyish delight at her appalled expression. Unable to think of a suitable reply to his decadent statement, Julia prodded Solomon into a trot. She should be furious at him, but his words, as wicked as they were, had pleased her. Had he really enjoyed tasting her as much as she'd enjoyed the pleasure he'd given her? He appeared at her side again, his expression unrepentant.

"Come now, Julia. I thought we had disposed of that prim and proper shell of yours last night."

"What occurred last night is not a subject for discussion here."

"I see. Then I shall call on you later this morning to further elaborate on the finer qualities of your honey pot, and the plans I have for filling it completely."

"*Morgan.*" She shot him a scandalized look while she struggled to maintain control of her growing arousal.

"Say that again." There was almost a note of tender possession in his gruff command.

"What?"

"Say my name as if I'd just made your honey flow hot and sweet."

"Dear Lord. Will you please stop?"

Her blood warmed by his scandalous words, the muscles below her stomach clenched then shuddered with a tiny spasm. She shot him a glance, and when his blue gaze met hers, she could see the passion glowing in his eyes. Morgan narrowed his eyes slightly before a look of surprise swept across his face. His hand flew out to grasp Solomon's cheek piece, and he pulled her horse to a halt.

"Sweet Jesus. You're hot and slick for me right now, aren't you?"

She swallowed hard at the desire tightening his jaw into a harsh line. Glancing away from him, she tried not to squirm in the saddle. Already her nether regions were screaming for his touch. If only she could arouse the same intense need in him, that he aroused in her.

With a daring she didn't know she possessed, she slowly raised her gaze to meet his. Deliberately, she wet her lips with her tongue, then met his gaze. Julia's confidence soared as she saw his jaw go rigid.

"Yes." She saw him swallow his tension in a violent bob of his throat. "Isn't that how you like me? Hot and wet on your tongue?"

The moment amazement settled on his face, Julia bit back her smile. It wasn't often one could silence Morgan St. Claire twice in less than twenty-four hours. His eyes narrowed on her as he shifted uncomfortably in his saddle.

"Take care, Julia. There are plenty of places here in the park for more than just a slight tryst." The hoarse sound of his voice thrilled her. He was as painfully aroused as she was.

"Indeed. Then I must guard my honey well until we meet again tonight."

Not waiting for his response, she lightly tapped Solomon's hindquarters with her crop and cantered away from Morgan. She'd actually matched wits with the man and bested him. Or at least not allowed him to think of a rebuttal. Invigorated by her daring, she smiled.

For once, she had gained the upper hand with Morgan St. Claire. She liked the way it made her feel. Powerful, witty, and feminine. Something she'd never felt before in her life. She'd shared control of their conversation and even managed to arouse him with her words.

Tonight, no doubt, he'd make her pay dearly for her behavior. The thought excited her almost as much as it surprised her.

Chapter 11

organ surveyed his bedroom. Everything was ready. All that was missing was the beautiful, seductive Julia. Earlier in the day, he'd sent her a note inviting her to dinner at seven. When she didn't reply, he'd considered sending another note demanding an answer. His misgivings were quickly eased the instant he recalled this morning's conversation.

The memory made him inhale sharply. Damn if the woman hadn't made him rock hard with just a few choice words. He grinned. Tonight he'd extract a delicious punishment from her. But he'd ensure that it was just as pleasurable for her as it was for him. Tonight was the night he'd been waiting for since he'd first set eyes on her nude portrait.

It had been a long time since any woman had captured his interest the way Julia had. Despite everything he did to push her out of his thoughts, she was always there. He tried to convince himself it was only lust talking, but it was becoming more difficult to think of her just in terms of his bed. Too often, he'd visualized her waiting for him when he came home from a long day at the office.

Home and hearth was something he'd avoided like the plague. The hellish existence of his childhood had taught him better. The life he led now was simple and enjoyable. No screaming matches, vile accusations or displays of affection that couldn't even warm an iceberg. Despite reassuring himself as to his choice in lifestyle, every time he thought of Julia, he found himself questioning his beliefs on the subject of marriage.

Here at the Clarendon, he could enjoy himself without the worry of his latest mistress thinking he might be persuaded into that state most women wanted to enter. But with Julia, his thoughts had wandered far enough off course to think about what it would be like to wake up with her each morning. He grunted with exasperation. Bloody hell, he was becoming far to enamored with Julia Westgard. The sooner he spent his lust for her, the better.

The clock began to chime the seven o'clock hour, and he glanced toward the door. As the timepiece chimed off a note for each hour, an unfamiliar jolt of apprehension made him tighten his mouth. Well, if she didn't come, he'd go to her. The thought had no sooner popped into his head than a quiet knock sounded on the door.

Eagerly he crossed the floor to let her into his suite. She stood in the corridor wearing a long evening cape with her face completely covered by a veil that deftly hid her features. Realizing she'd not wished to be recognized, he frowned. She'd been forced to cross the hotel lobby under censorious eyes. It was the one arrangement he'd failed to make for her arrival tonight.

"Damnation, I should have found a more discreet way for you to come here," he said in a gruff tone. It was the first time he'd ever regretted not having private lodgings.

"It's all right. I used the hotel's side entrance." She entered his suite and came to a halt a few feet into the main room. "It's quite discreet, but thank you for caring enough to be concerned for my reputation."

Relief drifted through him when he realized she'd not had to endure the curious looks from hotel guests in the lobby. The night of their wager, he'd thoughtlessly expressed a lack of concern for her reputation, and he bit down on the inside of his cheek. The last thing he wanted was for her to suffer any pain or criticism because of him. At least he'd had Henri prepare a cold buffet. It would eliminate the possibility of the hotel staff recognizing her. There would be no servants to spread gossip amongst the Set.

Her gloved hands unfastened the cape at her throat, and he helped her slide the garment off her bare shoulders. Unable to help himself, his fingertips brushed across her soft, smooth skin. Dressed in a emerald green evening gown, the silk garment hugged her body as though she'd been sewn into it. The neckline plunged downward into a vee, revealing the cleft between her breasts. Her veil still covered her face making her even more seductive and arousing. Clearing his throat, he waited quietly as she slowly rolled up her veil to reveal her lovely features.

His cock swelled in his trousers as she stared up at him. The sultry expression in her hazel eyes intensified the craving in his body. Almost as if she were aware of his reaction to her, she removed her gloves in a leisurely manner.

Unhurried, simple, and erotically seductive she peeled the elbow length silk off her arm. It left him battling the desire spreading its way through him. Bloody hell, he wanted to tumble her to the floor this second. No seduction, no teasing, just raw passion the driving force between them.

Morgan swallowed hard. He couldn't recall any woman ever igniting such an urgent need inside him the way Julia did. With any other woman he would have simply labeled his craving one of lust. But deep in the back of his mind, he'd already admitted that Julia was special. Somehow it he didn't think it would be as easy to let her go as he had other women. A small smile tilted the corners of her mouth. Even her amusement was enough to make him ache with need.

"Something smells delicious," she murmured as she glanced around the room. Unable to help himself, he leaned into her to breathe in her soft, tart scent.

"*You*, smell delicious."

"Said the lion to the lamb," she teased merrily with a laugh.

Although she met his gaze without flinching, he saw her fleeting look of trepidation. Wanting to put her at ease, he turned toward the buffet servers the hotel staff had brought upstairs.

"Come and satisfy your taste for whatever food you like."

As she moved to stand at his side, he lifted a silver dish cover. Julia immediately gasped with delight at the poached salmon arranged on the platter.

"You remembered," she exclaimed and looked up at him in surprise.

"I make it a point to remember everything about you." He smiled with satisfaction. Deep down inside he recognized it as happiness. It was a startling revelation.

"I think you remember what will serve you in some form or fashion at a later time," she said with a laugh.

Although her tone wasn't critical, he flinched at the observation. He didn't like the idea that she might really see him in such a light. Without answering, he gestured for her to fill her plate before following suit. Moments later, they moved to the small table set near the fireplace where Morgan pulled out her chair for her.

Chapter 12

A wave of heat enveloped Julia as she brushed past him and took her seat at the table. The sensation sent her heart skidding along at an alarming rate. It accelerated to a frantic pace as his fingertips trailed across the nape of her neck then along the top of her shoulder.

It was a feather light touch, but the effect on her senses was devastating. She darted a quick look at him only to feel the full force of his charm raining down on her as he offered her a wicked smile.

He'd scorned a jacket this evening, and the shirt he wore was open at the neck. Beneath the white linen shirt, his muscles rippled as he moved to take his seat opposite her. There was a relaxed air about him that spelled danger. But it was a danger she wanted to explore—if only for one night.

A comfortable silence fell between them as they ate, and she relished the poached salmon he'd ordered for her. He finished his meal first and reclined back in his seat to study her. The assessment in his eyes might have intimidated her weeks ago, but no longer. Although a wager had brought her to this point, she couldn't deny the truth. She wanted to be here.

The thought worried her slightly. Her attraction for Morgan was beginning to spiral out of control, making her all the more vulnerable to him. Shoving the thought aside, Julia reminded herself that it was for one night only. She had no intention of continuing this relationship beyond this evening. For one night she would enjoy the pleasure Morgan's touch gave her, while doing her best to tempt him as well.

"You really don't realize how beautiful you are, do you?" His unexpected observation made her jerk her gaze up to meet his quizzical one. She laughed with a healthy dose of disbelief.

"There it is again, that famous St. Claire charm. You have a way of making a woman feel as though she's the only one you've ever paid a compliment too." Her response made him frown for a moment, and once again, the flash of annoyance in his gaze puzzled her.

"Are you always so quick to dismiss someone's compliment? I *never* say something I don't mean, Julia." The quiet words sent a warm heat cresting up into her cheeks.

"Forgive me. I'm unaccustomed to being the recipient of any type of praise."

Silence hovered in the air between them, and she struggled to keep her expression serene as she saw the assessment in his warm brown eyes. The man had the ability to read her more easily than anyone she'd ever met. Her heart had slowed its pace during their meal, but it now resumed its frantic pace.

"Why did you do it?" His question startled her, and Julia shook her head in confusion.

"Do what?"

"The portrait. Why did you have Peebles paint you in the nude?"

The question made her throat close up, and she quickly reached for her wine glass in hopes of putting off his question. When she didn't answer, he folded his arms across his chest and eyed her with that piercing gaze of his.

"I'm waiting, Julia."

"I don't know that you'd understand," she said quietly as she set her glass back on the crisp damask tablecloth.

"Try me." The gentleness in his voice was soft and reassuring. Deep inside, something said she could trust him. She drew in a quick breath at the thought before she acquiesced to the instinct.

"I wanted to do something daring."

"An act of defiance?" His astute question made her curl up her fingers into a fist in her lap. She shrugged her shoulders.

"Perhaps. I know my husband would not have approved of my actions." A tiny sliver of satisfaction slipped into her consciousness. Oscar would have been livid.

"If I were him, I doubt I'd have approved either." The quiet response made Julia stiffen and clench her teeth .

"But you're *not* my husband, and Oscar's no longer here." She knew instantly she'd revealed far more than she'd intended. Morgan's eyes narrowed and studied her with an intensity that made her avert her gaze for fear of him seeing deep into her soul. She couldn't afford to give him that much power over her.

"Did you love him?"

"*No.* I—" She abruptly ended her vehement response. Desperate to change the subject, she hid the tumult inside her and met his gaze again. "It was a marriage no different from many others. And you. Why haven't you married? I would think you'd like a son to take over your business one day."

Others less observant wouldn't have noticed the sudden stillness about him that indicated he was immediately on guard despite his seemingly relaxed posture. There was a tension flowing through him that was almost tangible. He clearly hadn't been expecting the sudden shift of direction in their conversation. One elbow resting on the arm of his chair, his long fingers lightly rubbed against his chin as he studied her with an odd expression on his features.

"I suppose it's because there hasn't been a woman I liked well enough to ask." Something about his response made her heart skip a beat, but she ignored the unfamiliar sensation.

"Like." She tested the word on her tongue before nodding. "Yes, that would make the state of matrimony more agreeable, wouldn't it?"

It was a rhetorical question, and she watched as his forefinger tapped his firm, sensual mouth. A shiver of expectation raced across her skin at the memory of those lips on her sex. The nervous flutter that stirred in her belly made her hand tremble as she reached for her wine glass. The wine barely eased the dryness of her mouth.

"So you decided to be daring and had Peebles paint you, but that doesn't explain why you chose to make *me* your next adventure." His statement caught her off guard, and her eyes widened in surprise.

"I told you. I wanted to offer up your handkerchief for auction." As she recalled him bidding on his own handkerchief, she frowned with irritation.

"And you weren't expecting me to show up and bid on the item." His chuckle of amusement made her glare at him.

"It was unfair of you to bid against me."

"You set the terms of our wager. I simply saw to it that I didn't lose."

The grin on his face should have angered her, but it was impossible to be irritated when he looked like a mischievous boy who'd just gotten away with stealing a cookie.

"You're impossible," she huffed.

"Only when I don't get my way. But it still doesn't explain why you chose me, Julia." The deliberate note in his voice said he wasn't about to let her avoid answering the question. With a sigh of exasperation, she scowled at him. Why *had* she chosen to steal his handkerchief? The answer was simple. She met his gaze steadily.

"The portrait gave me a taste of what it was like to be daring. To take a risk. It was exhilarating, and I wanted to experience the sensation again. I knew your handkerchief would be a popular item at the auction, so I decided to steal it."

"It was a reckless thing to do," he growled fiercely. "Any other man might have forced you into his bed."

"Yes, but I'd seen how fair you are with the people who work for you. I knew you were an honorable man." He frowned and arched his eyebrows with skepticism. "Instinct told me that despite your reputation, I could trust you not to…to take advantage of me if I were caught in your room."

It was the truth. And he'd reinforced her opinion when he'd not demanded payment the minute she lost their wager. In fact, she was certain he would never have tried to coerce her into making good on her debt if she'd not been willing. And she was willing. Why else would she be here? She'd agreed to come here tonight not because of the wager, but because Morgan excited her.

In the back of her mind, she acknowledged the danger such a thought presented, but a familiar sensation flooded her senses. Exhilaration in its most potent form. Morgan had already shown her how thrilling his touch was, and tonight she intended to indulge her senses all she wanted. Just for this one night, she would allow herself the chance to experience what it was like to be in Morgan's bed. She could even attempt to seduce him if she wanted. Her skin grew warm at the thought.

"You put great faith in that instinct of yours," he said in a disapproving voice. "How I treat my employees doesn't reflect anything about me other than my belief that a happy employee is a productive employee."

"Are you going to deny that you're an honorable man?"

"That's not the point, Julia, and you know it." He glared at her. "You had no way of knowing I wouldn't seduce you the moment I found you in my bed chamber."

"What if I'd been the one doing the seducing?" She smiled at the look of astonishment on his face. "Do you think I'm incapable of seducing the great Morgan St. Claire?"

Arching an eyebrow, she stretched out her hand toward the plate of fruit sitting in the center of the table. She picked up a fat, luscious strawberry and dipped it into a small bowl of honey that sat next to the plate. The honey slowly edged its way down to the tip of the fruit, and she tilted her head back to catch the first drop in her mouth.

Her eyes caught Morgan's enthralled look. The desire blazing in his eyes pleased her. Tempting him gave her a sense of power. The sweet taste of control. The natural sweetener dripped onto her tongue. It was warm and sweet. Enjoying the taste of it, she swirled her tongue around the tip of the strawberry for more of the smooth, sticky treat. Then with a neat nip of her teeth, she bit off the bottom portion of the fruit.

The indistinct sound he made was part growl, part curse. His gaze bored into hers as he rose to his feet like a powerful lion ready to pounce. Her heart slammed against her breastbone. Whatever had made her even *think* she could seduce the man. She trembled as he stretched out his hand to her. The control she'd thought she had over him had been an illusion. She'd aroused his desire, but he'd never been out of control the entire time he'd been watching her.

The air around her seemed to pulse with a fury she was certain would consume her if she didn't take care. For the second time this evening, exhilaration pounding its way through her veins. Mesmerized by the raw passion in his riveting brown eyes, she laid her hand in his. His fingers closed over hers in a strong, but gentle grip as he pulled her to her feet and into his arms.

"You have a wicked streak in you, Julia."

She smiled at the gruffness in his voice. At least her effort to tease and tempt him had not been a clumsy one on her part.

"As usual, you exaggerate."

"*This* is hardly an exaggeration."

If possible, he pulled her closer to him then guided her hand down to his trousers and his erection. Startled by the feel of him beneath her palm, she shuddered as she met his intent gaze.

"My cock is hard for you, Julia. It won't be satisfied until its buried deep inside you."

The earthy rawness of his language sent excitement rushing through her limbs until need settled like a raging fire in her belly. The sensation spread its way into her blood, then downward even deeper until it permeated every one of her cells. Morgan swept her up into his arms and carried her down the corridor to his bedroom.

Less than a minute later, he set Julia on her feet and lowered his head to kiss her. It was a demanding kiss, and his teeth gently nipped at her bottom lip. The instant she gasped, his tongue swept into her mouth.

Claret tantalized her taste buds as his tongue swirled around hers until her knees wobbled. A muscular hand warmed the skin of her shoulder as his kiss deepened. It tugged at her, demanding a response and she gave it willingly. Her hands unbuttoned the front of his shirt, and tiny frissons slid across her skin as she touched the solid muscles of his chest.

Despite every warning she'd ever told herself about Morgan St. Claire, there was no doubt in her mind that this was an adventure she'd been longing for all her life. The skillful touch of his hands sent her dress sliding to the floor. Her corset followed the gown, but the only thing that registered in her mind was the dark, spicy scent, taste and feel of him. Cool air brushed her mouth as his lips danced across her cheek in search of first her ear lobe and then her neck.

An instant later, a large hand cupped her and his thumb brushed across the nipple beneath her silk chemise. With a low moan of pleasure, she trembled at the teasing caress. His mouth assaulted hers again as his thumb continued to circle round the stiff peak of her breast. It was heaven and penitence all in the same breath. Heaven to be succumbing to his wicked touch, while the intense hunger enveloping her body reminded her of every moment she'd resisted the pleasure of his caresses.

When his mouth captured her sensitive nipple through the thin silk of her chemise, another moan poured out of her. The wet heat of him suckling her ignited a wild passion inside her that demanded satisfaction. With a mind of its own, her body pressed into him eagerly. A sigh of bliss whispered past her lips as his mouth devoured a stiff nipple, and his thumb massaged and tweaked the other hard peak. Nothing she'd ever read or heard could have prepared her for the deliciously sinful sensations he aroused in her. Desire streaked through her veins, and the moment his teeth clamped gently down on the nipple, her insides grew slick with desire.

Fire streaked across her skin, and she instinctively reached for him, eager to satisfy the increasing ache inside her. Fingers flying over the waistband of his trousers, she freed his hard erection and grasped him firmly. The dark growl of delight rumbling in his chest vibrated against the fingertips of one hand, while his hips moved as he thrust his erection in and out of her grasp. The friction from his action burned pleasurably against her palm. Hard and thick, the thought of him sliding into her made her shiver with a mixture of trepidation and excitement.

Not once had her husband ever aroused her desire, but with only a few kisses, Morgan had ignited a wild craving in her. It sent her tumbling into a state of utter bliss with every kiss and caress. The powerful strength of the emotion made her heart pound against her breast. Did he know how easily she was her ready to give him whatever he asked of her.

Another shiver teased her senses, and she was filled with the overwhelming urge to feel Morgan's skin heating hers. With shaky fingers, she tugged at her chemise, almost frantic to remove all barriers between them.

Releasing her, he stepped back and swiftly removed the rest of his clothing as she discarded what little she still wore. Naked before him, she heard him suck in a sharp breath, and his hand cupped her chin.

"God, but you're beautiful." The palm of his hand caressed her throat before moving down past her breasts. When he reached her belly, a tremor went through her. "Are you hot and wet for me, sweetheart?"

His fingers dipped lower, and the instant he found her folds slick with a buttery cream, she jumped and released a soft moan. Triumph surged through him at her response. Tonight he would memorize every inch of her. Morgan kissed her again, lusting after the honey-sweet taste of her tongue.

With an eagerness that sent pleasure pulsing through his veins, she pressed her hips into him and her damp curls teased the tip of his cock. God almighty, he'd never expected her to behave with such wanton abandon. His gut twisted with desire the instant she wrapped her arms around him, her fingernails lightly razing the skin at the base of his spine as she murmured his name in an achy plea. He'd never heard a sweeter sound in all his life.

Eager to assuage their hunger for each other, he guided her backward until she sank down onto the edge of the bed. When she began to scoot back toward the center of the mattress, he stopped her.

"No," he rasped, gently forcing her to lie backward on the mattress with her legs hanging off the side of the bed. "I won't last long this first time, and I want to see your beautiful folds glistening with cream as I fuck you hard and fast."

Pink color stained her cheeks before her eyes took on a slumberous tilt. She stretched out her hand to trace her fingertips down past his stomach until they grazed across the top of his erection. Arousal evident on her face, the hunger shining in the depths of her eyes stole his breath away.

Christ Jesus, he was ready to come just looking at her. Quickly, he grabbed a nearby pillow, then slid his hands under her round buttocks. The fleshy underside of her was soft and full against his fingers as he lifted her off the bed slightly. With the pillow situated under her, it angled her upward until he could easily see her glistening folds.

Surprise swept over her face, as he wrapped her legs around his waist. His cock strained toward her wet heat until it was pressed at the entrance to her hot core. With one hard thrust he slammed his body into hers, filling her to the hilt. A loud, sharp cry of pleasure escaped her, and the silky legs wrapped around him squeezed at his waist in reaction to his possession.

Gratified by her response, his body rejoiced as he remained still inside her for a moment. God almighty, she was tight and fiery around his cock. A delicious sounding moan echoed out of her as she arched her hips up even higher in a silent plea for him to continue. The sight of her so aroused heightened his own desire.

Bending his head, he saw his erection coated with her hot cream as he withdrew from her, then thrust back into her once more. Slick with passion, her insides shuddered and clutched at his rock hard cock. Christ Jesus. The woman was about to make him come faster than an inexperienced youth.

His gaze flitted to her face. Eyes closed, her rapturous expression filled him with delight as he began to thrust in and out of her at a blistering pace. Her moans grew louder, which increased his ardor. Suddenly, her tight, creamy folds contracted around him in a hard spasm.

The sensations tantalizing his cock tugged a guttural cry from him as he began to thrust into her even faster. With each hot stroke into her slick core, her spasms tried to hold him inside, but he resisted her body's efforts to hold him still. The moment his cock demanded satisfaction, he slammed into her white-hot heat one last time, then lost his seed in one hard explosion.

Lodged inside her, his body throbbed with a pleasure he'd never experienced before. It was as if every woman who'd come before Julia had been obliterated in one simple act. His hands braced on either side of her, he drank in deep gulps of air as he enjoyed the slowly ebbing waves of their climax. He knew his body wasn't ready, but he wanted to take her again and again. What the fuck was happening to him? He'd never been this infatuated with a woman before. Luminous hazel eyes fluttered open to look up at him, and he swallowed hard. When in the hell had the tables been switched?

Chapter 13

Hands filled with food, Morgan turned around from the small table he'd replenished with dessert from the dining room. The sight of Julia in his bed filled him with more than just a sense of satisfaction, but he refused to examine the other emotions mixed in with what he was feeling.

Lying on top of the mattress with a red silk sheet entwined between her legs and pressed against her breasts, she was studying him with an expression of appreciation. As her gaze met his, he saw the flash of hunger in her hazel eyes. Exhilaration sped through his veins. It wasn't even the midnight hour, and they'd made love several times, yet his body craved hers as a drunkard did his wine.

"I take it you like what you see," he said with a grin.

"Very much."

The husky sound of her voice instantly made his cock stiffen, and he looked downward before he lifted his gaze to meet hers. A slight flush tinged her cheeks at the sight of his arousal, before she averted her gaze.

"You have that effect on me quite a bit." He chuckled as she blushed deeply. Crossing the floor, he set the food in his hands onto the night table next to the bed, then sat down on the mattress beside her. "Don't be ashamed of your power to incite desire, Julia."

"I'm—"

She didn't finish her statement as he tilted his head in a gentle, silent rebuke. Confident she wasn't about to protest any further, he grinned and gestured toward the bread, fruit, and cheese he'd brought to the bedside. A small smile curved her lips as she refused with a shake of her head. He studied her as her gaze drifted around his room almost as if she were seeking something.

Morgan followed her gaze, trying to see the room from her perspective. Paintings of several ships from his line adorned the walls, while a few trinkets stood on the mantelpiece. The room was devoid of any items that reflected who he was. For the first time, he recognized the true austere nature of his bedroom.

Its lack of anything distinctly personal suddenly made him realize the rest of his suite was equally stark. He'd never considered the subtly of his décor. Even here he'd unconsciously avoided adding too many things that might define his living space as a home.

His gaze swept over his bed. The red silk sheets and black bedspread shoved down to the foot of his bed were the only things that even remotely supported the reputation he'd earned as a heartbreaker. While he'd indulged in a number of affairs, Julia was the first woman he'd ever allowed into his inner sanctum. Morgan wasn't sure what surprised him more. The fact that he'd only just realized he'd never had a woman in his own bed before, or that Julia was the one he'd chosen to be the first.

"You're frowning," she murmured as she turned her gaze back to him.

"Am I?" He immediately ended his brooding and smiled at her before popping a grape into his mouth. The fruit was sweet on his tongue, although not as sweet as she was. She sniffed at his vague response, which made him laugh. "I assure you, I'm quite content at the moment."

It was the truth. He couldn't ever remember being so relaxed with any woman before Julia. While his desire for her was still strong, he was more than happy to simply sit beside her and enjoy the quiet peace he had discovered in her company. The strawberry he picked up from the platter reminded him of Julia's lovely red lips.

"Do you really find it pleasant or comfortable to live in a hotel?" Her question caught him completely off guard, and tension rocked his body as he swallowed his fruit.

"I'm sorry. I didn't mean to pry," she said gently. Avoiding her gaze, he stared at the fire crackling softly in the hearth.

"I have no need for a house. The hotel suits my needs, since I'm hardly here except to eat and sleep." The moment his words filled the air, he grimaced. Was there never going to be anything more to his life than work?

"Everyone has need of a home, Morgan," she said softly.

"Do they? Experience has taught me that a home is far from a happy place."

"Was your childhood that bad?" The question made him look at her.

"Bad enough to prevent me from making the same mistakes my parents did." He bit into another strawberry. "My father wanted nothing to do with me until I was old enough to take over the family business. My mother…my mother couldn't bear the sight of me."

"Dear lord." Her hand reached out to touch his chest in silent consolation. Although she didn't ask, he knew she was wondering why. He cleared his throat.

"At first, my mother couldn't stand to look at me because I was a reminder that she'd borne my father's child. With each passing year, my likeness to my father only made her distaste for me deepen."

"She must have hated your father very much." The sympathetic note in her voice offered him the same comfort as the warm hand pressed into his chest.

"There was a bitterness inside her that ate away at her until she died." He shrugged. "I grew up in the care of a nanny and later went to boarding school. I was happy there, and I rarely went home."

"What did you do for the holidays?" she asked with a soft gasp.

"As a rule, I stayed with friends or remained at school."

"It must have been very difficult for you, not having a real home to go to."

There was a quiet understanding in her words that made his jaw clench. The sudden longing for a place to put down roots swept through him with the force of a herd of stampeding cattle. It had been years since he'd experienced such a sensation. Morgan looked down at her and forced a smile.

"I survived," he said with a firmness that indicated he was through with the conversation.

Julia eyed him for a long moment as if testing his willingness to continue baring his soul. When he remained silent, the assessment in her gaze said she knew there was more to his tale than what he'd shared, but she made no further effort to question him.

With a movement that reminded him of a sleek cat, Julia shifted her body until she was lying on her stomach. Every inch of her called out to him until his fingertips tingled with the urge to touch her again. He was looking forward to seeing what she looked like in the soft morning light.

An image of waking up next to her for years to come flashed through his head. Alarm streaked through him. It was a ridiculous thought influenced by their conversation. The futile wish would vanish the moment he rid himself of this lust he felt for her. She was a tempting creature, and all evening long, he'd been amazed by her response to their lovemaking.

There would be many more evenings like this before they finally parted ways. Smiling at the thought, Morgan reached out to stroke her back. Her eyes were closed, and she smiled.

"That feels nice."

A strong desire to make her feel as content as he was made him begin to massage her back. Soft sighs of pleasure echoed from her, and he enjoyed her response to his touch. Pleasing her filled him with quiet satisfaction. Something he'd not experienced with any woman from his past. His hands slid down to the rounded globes of her buttocks. She tensed as his finger traced the line of her cleft then skated down the inside of her thigh.

She lifted her head and glanced over her shoulder to eye him warily. Trepidation glowed in her hazel eyes, and he leaned forward to kiss her lips. Retreating, he picked up the small pitcher of honey off the table beside the bed. He grinned at the puzzled look on her face.

"Something to make you sweeter." Brushing her hair off her back, he drizzled a thin stream of the natural sweetener over her lower back and across her round buttocks. Her gasp of surprise made him laugh. "Don't move or you'll make everything sticky."

"St. Claire, *what* are you up too?" She inhaled another sharp breath as his tongue lapped up a small section of honey from her skin.

"I'm enjoying a rare delicacy. Honey-laced Julia. Delicious."

Laughter rolled past her lips at the wicked amusement in his voice. The man was truly a rake, but a deliciously sinful one. The teasing play of his lovemaking simply reinforced the reason why so many women had fallen for him. What woman could resist such a man? She closed her eyes, enjoying the sensation of his tongue licking the honey off her skin.

Massaging fingertips slowly forced her legs further apart as he continued to eat the honey off the small of her back. With the slightest touch, his fingers slid along the inside of her thigh before they dipped between her folds. The instant he skimmed the edge of her sex, her body twitched and quivered at the caress. His teeth razed against one buttock before he gently nipped at her flesh while he slid two fingers into her in a smooth stroke.

Unable to help herself, a low moan escaped her. God, but the man knew how to please a woman. As he administered gentle love bites and leisurely strokes of his tongue to her buttocks, he applied pressure to a sensitive spot inside her. It wasn't the first time this evening he'd touched her there, and she loved the sensation of euphoria that rose inside her.

The man had caressed and teased her body over the last few hours as if he were a master musician playing a musical instrument. It was a seduction unlike anything she'd ever imagined. The need for more sent her rear arching upward as she pressed back against his strokes.

Familiar desire skidded wildly through her veins. For a brief instant, she wondered how she was ever going to walk away from him. Desire and need flung the thought aside. She started to roll over onto her back, but a firm hand held her in place.

"Not yet, my sweet beauty."

"Morgan, please. I want to feel you inside me," she whimpered.

"And so you shall."

His fingers increased stroking her insides, while alternating with quick flicks to the swollen nub in her wet folds. With every hedonistic touch, her buttocks arched up higher, pushing against his hand in a silent cry for fulfillment. His hand caressed her belly then easily pulled her up onto her knees, all the while continuing to stroke her with his heated caresses. Her insides ached with need, and she whimpered with hunger and a craving for him to bury himself inside her.

"Are you ready for me, sweetheart?"

"Oh God, yes." Was that hoarse cry really hers? Her body was on fire, and waves of excruciating longing crashed over her until she pleaded with him to end her suffering. "Please, Morgan, stop teasing me like this."

The suddenness of his possession made her release a cry of passion and surprise as he entered her from behind. Moaning with intense jubilation, she reveled in the sensations he aroused in her as he filled her completely. She wanted to weep from the strength of the pleasure cresting over her.

Stretched by his hard, thick length, it was the most hedonistic and rapturous thing she'd ever experienced. He started to retreat, and her muscles tried to clamp down on him in an effort to keep him inside her. Protesting with a quiet sound of disapproval, she pressed her bottom back into his hips, silently demanding he stay inside her for a little while longer.

In the next breath, he thrust back into her hard and deep, and she screamed with delight. Once again, he retreated, but this time the delay was shorter. With each thrust, he increased the speed of his strokes until his body pounded against hers with a frenzy that matched her own decadent need for fulfillment.

Hot lava rolled unhurriedly through her limbs toward her belly as she pushed back against his thrusts with unrestrained passion. Molten fire reached her belly, then erupted into rapid ripples of an exquisite climax. Her body gripped his, tightening and squeezing around him until he drove into her one last time, and with a loud roar of exhilaration spilled his seed.

The intensity of the moment as they shuddered in completion at the same instant blinded her to everything but the bliss his possession unleashed in her. Still buried inside her, Morgan leaned forward to kiss her back. When he finally withdrew from her, a languid lethargy sped through her limbs, and she slowly rolled onto her back to stare up at him.

"Thank you."

Her words seemed to please him, and he stretched out beside her. The moment Morgan's arm wrapped itself around her shoulders and pulled her close, she experienced a sense of contentment and happiness she knew wouldn't last. But she treasured it, nonetheless. Even though she didn't feel sleepy, she yawned.

"I think it's time for you to take a nap." He pushed a stray lock of hair behind her ear as he issued his order.

"I don't want to go to sleep. I want to make love all night."

"Insatiable minx." Chuckling, he kissed her brow. "I promise to wake you as soon as my body will allow."

"I'll hold you…" She yawned again, this time more widely and closed her eyes. "To that promise St. Claire."

His answer was to pull her close, and she reveled in the comforting sensation of her cheek burrowing into his chest. With his foot, Morgan kicked the sheet up into the air and caught it with his hand. The way he gently tucked the silk covering around them struck her as a tender gesture, and when he stroked her cheek, it made her sigh with contentment.

A warm body shifted against him as Morgan stared up at the ceiling. He glanced down at Julia's sleeping form. The sight sent a wave of inexplicable emotion coursing through him. For the first time in years, he actually felt happy. It was a strange sensation.

Lightly he trailed one finger down her cheek causing her to murmur something unintelligible. With great care, he slipped from her arms and slid out of bed. Retrieving his robe, he crossed the floor to the window. Small pinpoints of light sprinkled the dark sky as if the dawn was hours away, but he knew better from the clock on the mantle.

Julia had given herself to him tonight with a resplendent abandon that had thrilled and delighted him. The woman in the portrait had finally come to his bed, and she had exceeded his wildest expectations.

When they'd fallen asleep the first time, he'd promised to awaken her. But she was the one to wake first, and she'd massaged his cock until he ached to be inside her. The instant she'd mounted him had been an unexpected delight, and she'd ridden him with passion and exuberance until they'd climaxed together.

Afterward, they'd relaxed amidst the tousled sheets finishing the remnants of the fruit and cheese plate. For the first time since they'd met, she had appeared at ease in his company. Her quick wit and sharp mind, combined with her voluptuous body, made her a temptation he wanted to succumb to over and over again.

The memory of their lovemaking made his cock swell. God, he was hotter than hell for her just thinking about it. He swallowed hard as he struggled to keep from returning to bed and waking her. Bloody hell, he needed to control himself. This entire situation was spiraling out of control. If he wasn't careful, he'd wind up married to her.

He froze.

Married. He had no desire to marry. Did he?

The fact that he was questioning himself made him swallow hard. He turned his head to look at the woman in his bed. He'd set out to seduce her, only to discover he wanted something more. But marriage? Wouldn't it just be simpler to keep her as his mistress? No. She deserved better than that.

His back pressed into the wall beside the window, Morgan crossed his arms as he studied her intently from where he stood. A long time ago, he'd learned that the words marriage and happiness were completely incompatible. And yet, this woman made him think he was wrong. Closing his eyes, he visualized his life before Julia.

Long days merging into night as he toiled away at the shipping offices. He was a wealthy, successful businessman. But it held little meaning without someone to share it with him. It was a cold, lonely existence with the occasional heat of a mistress here and there. There was little genuine joy in his life. All of that had changed the first time he'd set eyes on Julia.

How was it possible to have fallen in love with her so quickly? So easily? The moment the insight flashed through his head, he jerked upright to stand rigid at the window. Love. It wasn't possible. Morgan St. Clair never fell in love with the women he bedded.

His gaze fell on Julia again as she stirred in her sleep. Closing his eyes, he could see every curve and sweet dimple of her body. And he loved her. The raw simplicity of it floored him. The portrait had merely intrigued him, but the woman had captured his heart.

Never in his wildest dreams had he ever imagined he would fall in love. The fact that he'd done so made him realize the inexorable truth. Deep down, he'd never given up on the thought of marrying and having someone to come home to.

No doubt, the Set would find it amusing that Morgan St. Claire had finally succumbed to the wiles of a woman. Then again, Julia wasn't just any woman. She was his. Tonight she'd come to him willingly and of her own free will. Not only had she come to him without coercion, she'd offered herself to him with a sweetness and passion that convinced him she had feelings for him.

Quietly, he returned to the bed. Slipping beneath the covers, he kissed her forehead with tenderness. The touch made her stir, and her eyes fluttered open.

"Morgan?"

"Shh, go back to sleep," he whispered.

"But I'm not sleepy, anymore." Her mouth parted in a wide yawn. Chuckling, he flicked her nose with his forefinger.

"Well I am, and I want to fall asleep, then wake up with you in my arms."

With another sleepy nod, she closed her eyes and burrowed into him like a sleek cat. He relished the sensation. Closing his eyes, Morgan listened to the soft, steadiness of her breathing. Tonight was the beginning of a future he'd never imagined possible. A heaviness filled his limbs as sleep slowly conquered him. Just before he sank into the peaceful dream realm, he smiled. Tomorrow he'd propose to Julia.

Chapter 14

Pink and orange trails of color glimmered outside the window as Julia quietly finished dressing. She would need to hurry or Morgan might awake. It would be disastrous if she were still here and that happened. He would no doubt try to stop her from leaving, and it would be difficult to resist him. He had a way of bending her to his will, and she couldn't afford to let him change her mind about ending their affair.

Glancing back toward the bed where he slept, she studied him for a long moment. She could have stood there for hours just watching him sleep, the way his chest quietly rose and fell from his steady breathing. In sleep, the harsh planes of his face had softened.

The lean hardness of his body was tangled in the red bed sheet, which had fallen to his waist. Her gaze caressed the muscular curves of his chest displayed so handsomely in the muted dawn light filling the room. Last night she'd adorned that steely torso with loving kisses. It was a memory she would cherish forever.

He stirred in his slumber, and a long, muscular leg thrust its way out from under the sheet to reveal the limb from foot to hip. The line of his thigh was beautiful. No artist could have created a shape so perfectly male. And there was nothing more dangerous than Morgan St. Claire and the unbelievable maleness of him.

Pain wrapped an icy band around her heart. She hadn't realized how difficult it would be to simply walk away from him. Swallowing the anguish swelling her throat shut, she pulled a piece of white silk from her beaded bag and laid it by his pillow. What would he do when he awoke? Would he be angry?

Of course he would. He'd be furious. The thought frightened her. Oscar had always made her pay dearly whenever she'd made him angry. She frowned as she chided herself. Morgan wasn't anything like her late husband. He'd not said or done anything to make her think she should fear him. It didn't matter. The sooner she left, the easier it would make things. There was no telling what he would do if she were still here when he awoke.

The thought of it made her quickly gather the last of her things. With one last look at him, she pulled her veil over her face. She wasn't just leaving Morgan—she was leaving her heart as well. It was something she'd not planned for. A soft sob whispered past her lips as she raced from the room.

Outside his window, the sounds of the city coming to life pulled Morgan from a deep sleep. Rolling over, he reached for Julia to pull her into his side. When his hands didn't find her softness, he shot up in bed. A quick glance around the room confirmed his fear. She was gone.

Damn the woman. He'd told her last night how he'd wanted to wake up with her in his arms. When was she going to learn he didn't like to be thwarted? He grinned. It was something he needed to get used too. Julia wasn't likely to become a meek and mild wife once they were married. But then he didn't want her any other way.

Tossing back the covers, he scrambled out of bed. As he did so, a white square of silk fluttered to the floor. A frown furrowed his brow as he bent to retrieve the material. The softly scented handkerchief bore the initials J.W.

Stunned, he stared at the monogram. It wasn't possible. Cold air cloaked his body as he sank down onto the bed. Numb to all sensation but the silk square he held, he rubbed the handkerchief between his fingers.

The softness of it disgusted him. It symbolized the view a large sector of society mistakenly held of him. A man whose affairs rivaled even Prince Edward's. He didn't give a damn about society, but he cared deeply about what Julia thought of him.

She must think him a true scoundrel if she actually believed him so callous as to leave a handkerchief every time he parted with a mistress. But then he'd allowed her to believe that ridiculous myth society had created. Otherwise, she wouldn't have taken the opportunity to silently declare their relationship null and void in such a calculated fashion. He'd always been entertained by the fictitious stories about his monogrammed handkerchiefs. The legend of how he ended all of his affairs by offering one of them to his lover to dry her eyes had been amusing. Until now.

Anger barreled through him as he snatched up his robe and shrugged it over his shoulders. Cinching the sash around his waist with a sharp tug, he paced the floor of his room. Damn her. She'd crept out like a thief in the night. But she sure as hell had left her damnable calling card. He crumpled the silk square in his fist.

It had been a long time since he'd been snubbed. He didn't like it one bit. Especially since he had every intention of marrying the woman. She was mad if she thought she could end things between them. She'd felt something last night. He was certain of it.

Her response to him throughout the night had been no act. Everything about her had been passionate, giving and above all, genuine. Julia cared for him.

She *had* too.

Roughly shoving a hand through his hair, he halted his pacing. He didn't want to consider the possibility that last night had meant nothing to her. If she'd come to him simply to fulfill the wager it would make what they'd shared sullied. Their lovemaking had aroused him not just because of her body, but also because of who she was.

He wanted more than just one night of passion from her. He wanted a lifetime of them. Then there were the quieter moments he craved. Those times when she wasn't aware of his gaze. When he could simply study her and be thankful, he was near her.

Bloody hell. He'd made a mess of things. He'd done everything he could to win her desire, but he'd done nothing to win her heart. What if that wasn't possible? Every muscle in his body ached with tension at the all too real possibility that she would not want him. He immediately rejected the notion.

No. He would find a way to win her heart. The alternative was unthinkable. With a grunt, he rang for a bath and readied his shaving tools. Julia was his, and he intended to make sure she understood they belonged together.

More than an hour later, Morgan's thumb pressed Julia's doorbell for a prolonged moment. As he eased up on the pressure, the door opened to reveal her butler. Almost immediately, dismay settled on Calvert's face.

"I'm sorry, sir. Mrs. Westgard is not receiving visitors."

"She'll see me."

"I am sorry, sir, but she made a specific point of instructing me not to let you into the house."

For a moment, he wasn't sure he'd understood the man, but one look at the uneasy expression on the butler's face told him he'd heard correctly. Damn the woman. If she thought to sway him from seeing her, she was quite mistaken.

"Calvert, I'm a reasonable man. I understand you're simply following instructions," he growled softly. "However, if you don't step out of my way, I doubt you'll be answering this door again any time in the foreseeable future."

He sent the man a look of grim determination. Threats were not to his liking, but no one was going to keep him from seeing Julia. Not even the woman herself. Calvert took a hasty step backwards. Nodding his approval, Morgan stepped into the small foyer and handed the other man his hat and cane. With sharp movements, he tugged his gray gloves off and dropped them into the soft felt homburg.

"Where is she?"

"The salon, sir."

In two strides, he was charging up the stairs and into the salon. Quietly, he closed the door behind him. She sat with her back to him at her desk, writing a letter.

"Who was at the door, Calvert?" she asked quietly. Although he couldn't be certain, the thought he heard a hint of fear in her voice.

"Good morning, Julia."

With a cry of surprise she sprang to her feet, knocking the chair over as she wheeled about to face him. The dismay on Julia's face didn't surprise him, but there was another emotion that shimmered in her gaze for a fleeting moment that sent a twinge of dread through him. He ignored the sensation and studied her for a long moment. She was beautiful. The yellow silk of her dress hugged her figure just as his hand had done last night.

No other woman had looked so alluring or tempting to him. Even with her lovely body completely hidden from his eyes, he remembered every inch of her. The woman had no idea how much power she wielded where he was concern.

Morgan would gladly give up everything he owned just to have her say yes to his proposal. Yes to a lifetime of happiness he'd never dreamed possible until he'd met Julia. Once they'd settled this small matter of his handkerchief, they were going to spend the day in bed where he'd convince her how much he loved her. The pleasant thought twisted his mouth into a small smile.

"How did you get in here?" Her eyes narrowed with anger as she studied him warily.

"I'm afraid I resorted to threats. Not a pleasant chore, but necessary given the rather unpleasant calling card I received this morning." Reaching into his coat pocket, he pulled out his silk handkerchief and dangled it in the air.

"Apparently you failed to understand the message. I've paid my wager in full. There will be nothing further between us."

The icy note in her voice made him frown. Where was the woman he'd made love to last night? The woman he wanted to make his forever. He studied her carefully. Her mouth was tight with tension, and despite her relatively calm demeanor, the fluttering pulse at the side of her neck belied her anything but serene state. He cleared his throat as he took a step toward her.

"That's where you're wrong, Julia."

Despite the furious glare she directed at him, her face paled considerably. One hand gripping the edge of the desk behind her, she squared her shoulders.

"You can't stand it, can you? You can't stand the fact that a woman had the audacity to reject you."

"*Damn it*, that's not the issue at all. You left me without an explanation of why."

"I don't owe you any explanation."

"I think you do," he said quietly. "What we shared last night was incredible. And I have no intention of letting that go."

"I refuse to join the St. Claire league of mistresses."

"Then marry me."

Julia stared at him in stunned silence, while ice sluiced through her veins. Mad, the man was stark raving mad. What on earth had possessed him to offer her marriage? The way he stood there so calm, so confident was enough to make her entire body ache with pain and longing. But it was her heart breaking that shook her badly. Part of her wanted nothing more than to fly into his arms and let him hold her.

Immediately she snuffed out the image. Last night had been a beautiful dream. It had made it easy to leave him while he was asleep. Her resolution to end their affair had been much easier to maintain at that point in time.

Now, having that penetrating gaze of his riveted on her, her resolve was shaky at best. And he'd proposed *marriage*. What possible reason could he have for doing such a thing? Flinching, she pressed her hands against her stomach in a vain effort to stop the wild emotions churning through her. His reasons were irrelevant. She had no intention of marrying Morgan St. Claire.

She would never marry again. Oscar had destroyed all her illusions about marriage with his cruelty and vile behavior. Marriage was nothing more than a prison. The thought had no sooner entered her head than her eyes focused on Morgan's face.

The firm set of his jaw showed how determined—how confident he was. It frightened her. He had a look about him that said he wasn't about to take no for an answer. It was cowardly, but all she wanted to do was escape. She couldn't help it.

She was terrified he might convince her to marry him despite all the reasons she shouldn't and couldn't do so. It would be even worse if he realized she cared for him. Erecting every barrier around her heart she could muster, she steeled herself for the battle to come. And it would be a battle. The stubbornness in his blue gaze assured her of that. She quivered as a muscle in his cheek twitched. He was a man on the edge. She could read it in the way he held himself.

"Usually when a man proposes, the woman responds." Morgan's voice echoed through the room as if a clap of thunder had reverberated directly over her head. She jumped. Dear lord, the man had been serious.

"You're delusional," she exclaimed.

"That was *not* the answer I was looking for."

"It's the only one you'll get," she said in a tight voice as panic flooded her limbs. With a sharp move, she swept past him on her way to the door. "Now if you'll forgive me, I've matters to attend too. Please see yourself out."

The safety of the salon door was almost within her reach when a powerful hand captured her wrist and pulled her to a halt. The heat sliding up her arm from his touch spread its way through her body with the speed of lightening. Gently, he turned her around to face him, his grasp still holding her in place.

Her gaze settled on the large, beautifully masculine hand that had carried her to the pinnacles of pleasure last night. Sweet heaven, she didn't want to pull away from him. Horrified by the realization, she fought to suppress the urge to fall into his arms. There was an implacable gleam in his eyes as he met her gaze steadily.

"I want you to leave, St. Claire." With a jerk, she tugged free of his hold and glared up at him.

"So you're willing to forget everything that's passed between us. Last night even?"

The gruff note in his voice made her mouth grow dry. There was a tenderness in the sound that shook her resolve more than anything he could ever say to her. He was right. Last night had been a night she would cherish the rest of her life. Passion, tenderness, and happiness had been hers for a few short hours.

If he had insisted she become his mistress, she wouldn't have been astonished one bit, but *never* in her wildest imaginings had she expected him to propose marriage. It was unbelievable. Worse, it frightened her because deep inside she wanted to say yes. Terrified by the thought, her fingers crushed the delicate yellow silk of her gown in her fisted hands.

"Last night meant nothing to me," she lied. Her firmly spoken words hung in the air like a sharp pendulum swaying between them ready to slice one of them in two.

"Don't lie to me, Julia," he snarled. "Last night *did* mean something to you. It meant something to both of us."

"I'm sorry, but you're mistaken."

"The *hell* I am. You're hiding behind that cool façade again, and I think it's because you're afraid."

"You're *wrong*."

Her heart skipped a beat. Was her fear so obvious? He bent his head toward her, and she hastily stepped backward until she found herself braced against the door. He immediately pressed his advantage, his hard hands grasping her shoulders. Despite his obvious frustration, his touch was firm, yet gentle, as he kept her from fleeing. He narrowed his gaze at her.

"You're terrified, and I think it's because I made you feel something last night."

"Really, St. Claire. You think too highly of yourself." She clenched her jaw at the way he flinched.

"You forget whose bed you slept in last night." His forefinger traced a feather-light trail down her cheek. "You're a woman of deep passions, Julia. Last night you showed me the woman in the portrait."

"No," she said in a tight voice. "It was an illusion. You saw what you wanted to see."

"Is *this* an illusion?"

The swiftness with which he bent his head and slanted his mouth over hers stole her breath away. The expert way his tongue teased her lips apart made her shudder with desire just as she had last night. Sweet heaven, if possible her body hungered for him even more than she had only a few short hours ago.

The scent of him was maddening. Spicy hot with a hint of cedar. Last night he'd driven her over the edge with passion, and his kiss now emphasized how that would never change. She would always feel this craving for his touch. The knowledge that she would never be kissed by him again horrified her, and her resolve to resist him weakened. His mouth nipped at hers until a soft moan rippled from her throat.

Unable to push herself away from him, she could feel her willpower eroding with each second she was in his arms. His touch set her on fire until her body was crying with a need that surpassed what she'd experienced with him last night. Another moan broke past her lips as he caressed the side of her neck with his mouth.

"I want you, Julia. I want to feel your fiery heat clutching at my cock as I slam into you over and over. I'm never going to get enough of you."

The seductive words escalated the desire unfolding inside her. Sweet Lord. When he talked like that, it excited her. Despite every logical reason not to, she relished his masterly behavior, the way he commanded her to kiss him or touch him.

He did so in a way that convinced her he was also thinking of her pleasure, not just his. Tiny frissons skated over every inch of her as his hands undid the front of her dress. Warm fingers stroked her skin, and she shuddered beneath the touch. She didn't want to feel this desire, this craving, but it was impossible to shut her feelings off where he was concerned.

A familiar, wet heat settled in the sensitive area of her sex, and her belly tightened with desire. As he unbuttoned her dress almost to her waist, she whimpered at the way her breasts ached for his touch. Dear lord, she was desperate for his mouth on her. He nibbled at her skin where the tops of her breasts rounded up at the edge of her corset.

"Christ Jesus you taste good," he rasped. A large hand tugged her closer until his erection pressed intimately through the layers of clothing against her thigh. "See what you do to me, Julia. I know you want me as badly as I want you."

There was a note of confidence in his voice that broke through the haze of passion clouding her head. Her arousal was blinding, but a tiny voice of reason whispered through the fog of desire. If she didn't stop him now, there would be no turning back. The struggle to give in to her passion tore at her heart. If only she could give herself to him once more. If only she had the courage to take that risk. To do as he asked.

But she didn't. She had to stop this mind-numbing passion from consuming her entirely. If it continued, she'd be lost for certain. She would lose the small wedge of independence she'd achieved since Oscar's death. *That*, she would not give up.

Desperately she tried to push her way up out of the depths of the passion engulfing her. His hands moved against her skirts and a cool brush of air blew across her calves. Frantic to stop him and end this blissful, but dangerous interlude, she tried to push his hands away from her.

Her resistance simply resulted in him pressing her against the back of the door with his body. With ease, he caught her hands and pinned them over her head. It was a position of complete control. Utter domination. Exactly like the terrible moments her husband had tied her up to prevent her from moving. The memory made her mind go numb.

Desire fled in a heartbeat. Morgan's action revealed him for the man he was. He intended to take what he wanted. He was no different from her husband. The thought clutched at her chest painfully. For the first time she understood just how much trust she'd placed in him. It was why she'd been able to be with him as she had last night. Somehow, he'd made her feel safe, but she'd been wrong to trust him.

Frantic to escape, she tried to pull her hands free of his powerful grip. His strength overpowered her. The futility of it layered her skin with a coat of ice as if a bucket of freezing water had been dashed in her face. It was happening all over again.

The pain. The humiliation. The degradation. Harsh emotions ate away at her and whirled a chaotic path through her body. She'd thought Oscar's death had meant she would never feel this sickening feeling again, but here it was, welling up inside her like a flood.

Tears she never thought to shed again welled up inside her, and she squeezed her eyes shut. She would not shed tears over him. How foolish she'd been to think he wasn't like Oscar. And she had. She'd actually thought him different. When they'd made love last night—*no*, she didn't want to think about last night. It had been nothing more than a dream.

Revulsion and fear gnawed at her as she froze beneath his touch. His mouth sought hers, and she didn't respond to his kiss. He could dominate her physically, but he would never rule her thoughts. Helpless to stop him, she knew the only way to shut out the pain and humiliation was to close her mind off to everything around her.

Self-preservation forced her to wrap an all too familiar cloak of indifference around her heart and soul to wait until the storm had passed. It was a form of mental survival she'd practiced far too many times with Oscar. She didn't protest. Protesting only increased the pain and cruel torment. She simply went limp in his arms. Turning her face away from him, she waited. It would be over soon enough.

Chapter 15

Nibbling at her ear, Morgan pressed his hips into Julia's. Damn, he was ready to spill his seed any minute. His cock throbbing for release, he drank in her faint lavender scent. He would never be able to smell lavender again without thinking of her. If he could only make her see how much she meant to him. How the sight of her made him want to forget the world completely.

Falling asleep with her in his arms this morning had given him a peace he'd never experienced before in his life. It had felt as though he'd been on a long, difficult voyage and had finally reached safe harbor. Eager to show how much she meant to him, he sought her mouth with his. She didn't turn her head to meet his kiss. Instead, she remained motionless.

A thread of surprise wove through him as he explored the soft skin of her cheek. With his free hand, he tenderly caressed her throat down to her shoulder and paused. Something was wrong. He lifted his head and frowned. Her profile resembled a skillfully crafted marble statue, while the tension in her muscles held her rigid and unyielding.

Concern rapidly suppressed his desire as he realized how icy her skin was beneath his fingertips. Pulling away from her slightly, he captured her chin and turned her face toward him. Her gaze was glassy and completely devoid of emotion. She'd retreated from him. Physically and emotionally. Fear coiled tight in his chest as he stared down at her. God help him. Had she really meant what she'd said? Had last night meant nothing to her?

"What is it, sweetheart? What's wrong?"

"Do what you like, then release me."

"*What?*" He jerked his head backward as if she'd slapped him. "*Christ Jesus*, I will not take you against your will, Julia."

"Isn't that what you're doing now?" There was an inhuman vacancy to her voice as she stared right through him. "You pin me against the door. Confine my hands. What else am I to think?"

His blood ran cold, and he quickly put several feet between them and watched her slowly lower her hands from over her head. How could she think all he wanted to do was rut? He'd been excited—eager to touch her. Eager to assuage his desire, *and hers*. It would always be like that for him. He'd never be able to get enough of her. Whether in bed or just being close to her, she was everything to him.

"I'd *never* hurt you." He bit out with a growing fear that held him stiff as he studied her pale features.

Guilt pounded him at the thought he'd made her think he would force himself on her. She turned her head away from him and remained silent. One hand clutching her wrist, she rubbed it in a manner that enhanced his shame. Shock held her beautiful features taut, and his body ached as if he'd taken a punch to his midsection.

He'd hurt her, and he'd just said he never would. His throat closed up at the thought. Last night she'd been warm and passionate in his arms, but today he barely recognized her. Where had the woman in the portrait gone? What had made her disappear? His mind raced along in search of an answer.

Westgard. Her husband was behind this. Morgan was certain of it. Over dinner, every time Julia had mentioned her dead husband, there had been a tension in her that said her marriage had been less than happy. But her reaction just now suggested there was something else behind the strain he'd witnessed in her last night at the brief mention of her husband. What the hell had Westgard done to her?

"How did he hurt you?" His harsh demand made her flinch, and she avoided his gaze as she shook her head.

"It doesn't matter. He's dead now."

"The *hell* it doesn't."

He grimaced at the way his fierce tone made her recoil. With great effort, he controlled the fury rising inside him at the thought of Westgard hurting her. Determined to know the truth, Morgan kept his voice quiet and controlled as he studied her.

"Tell me what he did to you, Julia."

At his demand, all hint of color drained from her face. Sheer will power was the only thing locking every muscle in his body as he fought not to go to her. Morgan's gut twisted viciously with a need to hold her and make her feel safe. But he knew without a doubt, it would only make matters worse. Instead, he waited in silence for her to speak. Not looking at him, she inhaled a deep breath, and her features seemed to pale even more, if possible.

"He would tie me to the bed, while he…he did things to me that…"

"*Christ Jesus*," he rasped.

The torment on her lovely face ignited a violent fury inside him for what she'd suffered. Certain his rage was visible on his features, Morgan quickly turned away from her, afraid he might frighten her more than he already had. Westgard was fortunate to be dead. If the man were still alive, Morgan would have slowly tortured the man to death for abusing Julia. He'd always known there was something driving her to hide behind her cool exterior, but he'd never imagined something this disturbing.

A chill swept through Morgan. He'd been the catalyst for bringing her painful memories to the surface. He shoved a hand through his hair. The idea that she associated his behavior with things her bastard of a husband had done to her twisted Morgan's gut with excruciating misery.

It was little wonder she'd fought him every step of the way over the last few weeks. He would have to tread carefully. Making her understand he wasn't like Westgard would take every bit of patience and diplomacy he possessed. Morgan turned to face her, and the look of anguish on her sweet features made him ache. It was clear she was near a breaking point, and he was at a loss as to how to ease her pain.

"Julia, I'm not like Westgard," he said softly. Julia didn't react, she simply kept her gaze focused on the floor. He tried again. "I want to marry you. I want to make you happy."

"*No.*" The harsh rejection was as painful as a kick in the teeth would have been.

"Listen to me," he pleaded. "I will never do anything to hurt you. I swear it."

"I…I cannot. Please don't ask it of me." The hint of indecision in her tone gave him hope, and it was enough to make him throw caution to the wind and risk everything.

"Would it make a difference if I told you…if I…" Morgan stumbled over his words. "If I said I loved you."

For a moment, he didn't think she was even going to look at him. Silently, he willed her to do so as his taut muscles ached from the tension flowing through him. She lifted her head slowly to meet his gaze, and his mouth went dry with fear. Hazel eyes dull and vacant, she shook her head slowly.

"I will never marry again."

"Julia, you can't—" Even to his ears, he could hear the desperation in his voice as she lifted a hand to stay his protests.

"I want you to go now. I don't want to see you any more."

The flat, emotionless words lashed out at him like a bullwhip. He wished they had been a whip. The sting would have been far less painful. What the hell was he going to do? What could he say or do to make her believe he wasn't like Westgard? That he'd give his life to keep anyone, including himself, from harming her. Dazed, he shook his head.

"I'll go, for now—but I've not given up on us."

"I'm sorry, Morgan. I won't change my mind."

He flinched at the finality of her words. The resolve on her face was just as unalterable. He flexed his jaw with frustration. This wasn't over as far as he was concerned. She needed time. He'd give her that. But in the end, he'd find a way to make her see they were meant for each other. He had to. If he didn't, he would lead a bleak existence without her.

Chapter 16

The Lyceum Theatre was hot and noisy as Julia took her seat next to Catherine in the Westgard box. Mrs. Langtry was performing in Antony and Cleopatra tonight, and the theater was more crowded than usual. With a flick of her wrist, she opened her fan and stirred the air in front of her.

Peacock feathers brushed across her nose as she leaned forward to see if Prince Edward was in the Royal Box. She chided herself. It wasn't the Prince she was hoping to see. She knew Morgan had a box at the theater, but she wasn't certain where. It had been little more than a week since that terrible scene in her salon.

At the time, she'd not been able to separate Morgan's behavior from her experiences when Oscar had been alive. But in the days that followed, she'd come to realize how pained Morgan had been at having caused her distress. As if he understood how upset she'd been, he'd made no effort to contact her until this morning when a small bouquet of hyacinths had arrived.

The meaning of the purple flowers was not lost on her. Morgan had been silently expressing his sorrow and regret. The flowers said he understood how his desire had triggered unpleasant memories for her. But it had been more than a conciliatory gesture on his part as there had been a single red rose included in the bouquet. The symbol for love had tugged at her heart as she'd extracted the flower and placed it in a vase by itself.

Was it possible he really did love her? Morgan's declaration of love almost a week ago had shaken her to the core. The moment he'd said he wanted to marry her because he loved her, had almost broken through Julia's defenses. But she'd sent him away instead. In the hours and days that followed, she'd found herself wondering if she'd made a mistake.

As she had for the past week, she dismissed the question. It didn't matter what Morgan's feeling were or hers for that matter. It wouldn't change her thoughts on marriage. It wasn't a risk she was willing to take, no matter how much she loved him. Sinking back into her chair she sighed softly.

"You've been quite the hermit this past week." Catherine sent her a look of curiosity. "Is there something wrong?"

"Not at all." She forced a serene smile to her lips.

"I see. Then perhaps you could explain why St. Claire is watching you from across the way with such pained hunger."

Startled, she stared at her cousin for a moment before Julia followed the other woman's gaze to the boxes on the opposite wall of the theatre. Morgan sat almost directly across from her, his eyes watching her every move. Her heart skipped a beat at the sight of his handsome face. Even from this distance, she saw the tension in his body. He looked tired. Sweet heaven, had he had another migraine episode? She hated the thought of him suffering.

Her gaze met his, and the intensity of his look warmed her body in a brief second. A flood of emotion surged through her, and she hastily turned her head away. How she wanted to give in to impulse and go to him.

"Well?" A gentle concern darkened Catherine's eyes. "Are you going to tell me what's going on between the two of you?"

"There's nothing between St. Claire and me. I'm simply an investor in his company."

"Really, my dear, you can try convincing yourself of that fact, but I saw the look you just gave him. You're in love with the man."

Stunned, she stared at Catherine in horrified amazement. If her cousin could see she was in love with Morgan, would he be able to tell as well? A layer of ice skimmed over her skin. It had been hard enough to send him away, but if he knew she loved him, he would be relentless in his pursuit.

"You're mistaken. I am not in love with Morgan St. Claire." Even to her ears, the words sounded hollow. Catherine studied her for a long moment, her eyes sympathetic.

"He's not Oscar, dearest."

"I don't know what you're talking about." She turned her head away and fanned herself a trifle too quickly before she realized how it might appear and slowed her hand movement to maintain her stance of indifference.

"Morgan St. Claire is a good, honorable man, Julia. He's far and away a better man than your husband ever was."

"That may be true, but I refuse to let him, or any man, dominate me again. The humiliation of it…" She closed her eyes at the painful memories swirling in her head.

"Oh, Julia, you cannot allow Oscar's beastly behavior to deny you the chance for some happiness. That monster turned a young, vibrant girl into a reserved woman who's afraid to live, but I've seen glimpses of that girl since his death."

"I am not afraid to live. I've been quite adventurous of late—scandalous, in fact." There was a note of bravado in her words that made her cousin send her an arched look.

"Having an affair is not the same thing as living," Catherine said quietly.

Silence filled the theatre box as Julia met her cousin's sympathetic gaze. She swallowed her embarrassment as she tried to find her voice. "How did…who else knows?"

"There's been a small amount of talk, speculation really. I wasn't even certain myself until just a few moments ago when I saw the way the two of you looked at each other."

"It's over," she said tersely.

"Is it?" Catherine reached over and touched her arm. "From your reaction, I'd say it was far from over."

"I cannot and will not allow myself to let any man control me ever again. The price is too high."

She bit her lip at the thought of giving herself up to Morgan's control. He *was* different from Oscar. Logic told her that. But emotionally, she did not want to face the prospect of giving up command over her own destiny.

"Is that what really frightens you, or are you afraid to risk trusting him *and* yourself?" At Catherine's query, she turned her head toward the other woman, then shook her head in disbelief.

"Are you suggesting that I open myself up to such a risk?"

"What I'm *suggesting* is that you trust yourself to be with him simply because he makes you happy.

"It's…it's impossible." She snapped her feathered fan closed with an abrupt movement.

"Happiness is never impossible once you choose to accept it." Catherine smiled at her gently as the house lights dimmed. "It's the trusting that's difficult."

The soft words whispered through her head as the curtain rose and she tried to focus on the performance. Catherine had no idea how difficult it was for her to trust. Once she had been able to trust herself and others, but Oscar had changed all that.

She wanted to trust Morgan. It was something she wanted desperately. But trusting him meant believing he would never hurt her. She wasn't certain she had that much trust within her to give. But if that were true, then how had she been able to trust him each time he touched her.

In her heart, she knew he would never force her to do anything she didn't want to do. He was first and foremost a gentleman. Last week, he could have easily taken her by force, but he'd stopped. A lesser man would have seen her submissive behavior as a signal to do as he liked.

Not Morgan, he'd known something was wrong by her lack of response. Time and again, he'd proven how considerate he could be toward her. How attuned he was to her pleasure. Although it had taken several days to recover from the shock of that last encounter, he'd clearly demonstrated his respect for her feelings.

Morgan didn't want her submissive. He'd said he wanted the woman in the portrait Peebles had painted, and she believed that now. But did she have the ability to be that woman? Did she have the courage to open herself up to him in such a manner? Perhaps Catherine was right.

Could it be she needed to choose happiness? Was it as simple as choosing to love him—to be with him? They didn't need to be married to be happy. And she cared little what society thought of her behavior.

Torn with indecision, her gaze drifted across the width of the theater to find Morgan watching her still. Instantly, the entire world slipped away as they stared at each other. There was nothing but the two of them. He leaned forward a small fraction as if he thought it might be possible to reach out across the void and touch her. Then he stiffened and reclined back into his seat.

Morgan ached as if he'd been in a street brawl with a group of sailors. He'd never experienced this type of torment before in his life. It was an all-consuming need for a woman, and his treatment of her had done nothing to advance his suit with her. The memory of how she'd retreated from him in her salon last week gnawed at his gut.

In his eagerness to convince her they were meant for each other, he'd dredged up unpleasant memories instead. He should have realized long before she'd come to his bed that Westgard had mistreated her. All the signs had been there, but his lust had blinded him to them.

Christ, to think that son of a bitch had tied her up. He was afraid to think what else the bastard had done to her. Her expression that morning was one he would never forget. The woman he'd made love to the night before had vanished. In her place was a woman completely detached from her emotions and from him.

Even now, the thought of what Westgard had done to Julia disgusted him. She had to be one of the most courageous people he'd ever met. Hell, it was amazing she'd even had the courage to give herself to him. Their lovemaking had built a fragile bridge of trust between them, and he'd unwittingly broken that bond.

He needed to do something that would reassure her, rebuild that tenuous connection between them. But what? Closing his eyes, he suppressed a groan of despair. Damn it to hell, he needed to do something. Anything. He looked across the theater again.

To his amazement, she was watching him. As their eyes met across the distance, she abruptly jerked her head back toward the stage. God, she looked beautiful. But vulnerable too. Was that his doing? Had he shattered that ice shell of hers to reach the woman Westgard had tried to destroy?

His fingers dug into his thighs as he struggled to remain seated. All he wanted to do was charge over to her box, scoop her up into his arms and take her home with him. The image of his hotel room filtered its way into his head. It was all wrong for her. Julia needed a place where she could feel safe and in control. His hotel room was the last place she would be able to do that. No, she needed something more stable, more tangible. For the first time he wished he had a house.

Until now, the hotel had served his needs more than adequately. It had also been a suitable deterrent to any mistress attempting to put her own stamp on any house he owned. But he also knew he'd been resistant to a house because of what it represented. Or didn't represent. A home. If he could give Julia all the safety, comfort, and warmth only a true home could offer, perhaps that would show her how much he loved her. The question was whether or not she'd be willing to share it with him.

Applause sounded in his ears, and as the lights went up in the theater, he realized it was intermission. In the box opposite him, he watched as Julia leaned toward the woman beside her. He had to see her. Hear her voice. Impulse drove him to his feet and out of his box. Despite the crowd surging out into the lobby in search of refreshments, he was able to reach Julia's box in just a few moments.

Pushing the curtain aside, he found her alone. Uncertain as to what his reception would be like, he cleared his throat. The moment he did so, she turned her head toward him. Pleasure flashed in her eyes before her expression became guarded. She didn't say anything, and clearing his throat again, he bowed.

"Good evening, Julia."

"Good evening."

There was a breathless quality to her voice that stirred his hunger for her. Since he'd left her salon last week, he'd filled his days with work, but his nights had been cold and restless. Morgan knew Julia needed time and distance between them, but he'd held out hope she would visit the shipping office to continue reviewing his books. As each day passed without her appearance, his misery had deepened. Now, staring at her, Morgan was suddenly at a loss for words.

"Did you receive my flowers?"

"Yes." She hesitated slightly. "It was…it was thoughtful of you."

The tension between them edged its way over his skin like a hot knife. He'd not felt this awkward in years. He stood in the box wondering what to say next.

"May I?" Morgan gestured toward the empty chair opposite her.

She hesitated again before she gave him an abrupt nod. Seating himself beside her, he studied her for a long moment. Although she projected a look of serenity, the frantic flutter at the side of her neck revealed her nervousness. Her gown was the color of the sea and made her look like a lush water nymph. The material hugged her full curves seductively, and his hands ached to caress her roundness.

"Must you stare?"

"What would you have me do? Kiss you instead?" he asked softly, then silently cursed his impatient nature.

Pink color tinged her cheeks as she blew out an exasperated breath. Her reaction to his words sent hope barreling through him. Opening her fan, she waved the feathers in front of her in an agitated fashion.

"I…you should not be talking to me like that."

"Perhaps, but it gives me great pleasure to see you're not indifferent to me." He bit back a smile as she slapped her fan closed with an annoyed twist of her lips.

"Don't be ridiculous," she snapped. Leaning forward, he slowly stroked the top of her knuckles with his forefinger. She trembled beneath his light touch.

"Then tell me you feel nothing when I touch you."

"I…I do not." She paled slightly and turned her head away.

"Do you want to know what I feel when I touch you like this?" he murmured as he caught her hand in his. "I'm on fire for you."

Julia quickly turned her head to look at him, a tiny gasp parting her lips. The moment their eyes met, he was certain he saw desire flash in her hazel eyes. Julia's hand still in his, Morgan turned it over so he could stroke her bare skin through the circular opening of her evening glove. The sharp breath she drew in at his touch sent tension rocking through him.

"Please don't," she whispered.

"Don't what? Tell you how much I adore you?"

"How could you possibly feel that way? We barely know each other," she said with breathless exasperation.

"I know enough that I want to spend the rest of my life with you."

She didn't say anything. She just stared at him for a long moment as if debating how to reply. For the briefest of moments, he was certain she wanted to tell him the same thing. But with a sudden shake of her head, she looked away.

"I told you before that I'll never marry again." Her quiet words made his jaw tighten with frustration. Westgard had done his work well.

"I refuse to give up on you, Julia." Once more, he stroked the skin of her wrist with his finger. "I don't have a choice. I need you as much as I need air to breathe. Every part of me aches for you. You have no idea how much I want to be kissing every inch of you right now. Touching you until you cry out my name as you flow hot and sweet over my tongue."

"Morgan, please."

Her whisper was almost inaudible, but it was clear his words excited her. Their gazes locked, and he sucked in a sharp breath. The same feverish need burning inside him was glowing in her beautiful eyes. She wanted him. Raising her wrist to his mouth, he pressed his lips to the small area of bare skin her evening glove revealed.

"Let me take you home." He watched her struggling to make a decision, her expressive face conveying all too clearly the battle raging inside her.

"I…that's not possible."

"Let me show you we're meant for each other, Julia. Let me show you how much I love you." The moment he said the words, he realized he'd pushed too hard. Julia paled then shook her head and inhaled a deep breath as she met his gaze steadily.

"Time won't change my mind, Morgan. All I want is to be left alone."

Frustration slammed into Morgan at her refusal to give way, and he abruptly released her hand to recline back into his seat with a grunt. Silence fell between them for a long moment, before Morgan leaned forward.

"I'm a patient man when I want something, Julia. I'm willing to give you time, but be forewarned. This is not the last you've heard in this matter."

Her lips parted as if she were about to say something, when the sudden swish of the curtain behind him stopped her. Rising to his feet, he turned and bowed as the woman he'd seen with Julia earlier entered the opera box. Julia quickly introduced him to her cousin in a manner that indicated she was clearly agitated by his words. With the introductions complete, he bowed over Julia's hand.

"Remember what I said, Julia," he whispered against her fingers. With that, he excused himself and left the box. Despite his disappointment at having lost this particular battle, something told him it was possible to win the war.

Chapter 17

ulia frowned at the figures in front of her. This was the second time she'd found something amiss with the Sea Witch's logs. Nothing added up correctly, and it concerned her enough to bring it to Morgan's attention. With a frown, she worried her lip with her teeth. It had been a week now since she'd seen him at the Lyceum Theatre.

No, that wasn't quite true. She *had* seen him. He'd passed her several times in the shipping office either in the main workroom or in passing as one of them arrived or departed. Each time he'd greeted her with a courteous nod and nothing more. He was doing exactly what she'd asked him to do the night she'd seen him at the Lyceum.

So why did the fact irritate her so much? For a man who professed to care for her, and stated emphatically he wouldn't give up his pursuit of her, Morgan was certainly not working very hard to change her mind.

Dismayed by the direction of her thoughts, she pulled in a sharp breath. Had she gone mad? The last thing she wanted was for Morgan to continue pursuing her. It was bad enough she found it difficult to hide her body's reaction to his presence whenever he was near her.

With one silk-edged word, Morgan could easily have her eating out of the palm of his hand. And it terrified her to admit that she wanted to do just that. She wanted to give herself over to him completely. The traitorous thought made her slam the ledger closed.

Glaring at the accounting book, she pressed her fingers into its cloth binding. The discrepancy in the Sea Witch's log needed his attention. Prepared or not, she needed to prove to herself that she could control her emotions where he was concerned. Despite what Catherine had said about seeking happiness, she firmly believed her refusal to indulge in a continued liaison with Morgan was the best course of action.

With a quick step, she left the small office Morgan had provided for her use. A moment later, she was standing in front of his office door. Hesitation stayed her hand briefly before she rapped on the wood. Hearing his command to enter, she inhaled a deep breath, and stepped into the lion's den with the ledger clutched tightly to her breast.

Morgan was standing at the window as she entered his office. A look of surprise darkened his blue eyes when he turned his head toward her. Abruptly, he wheeled about and strode to his desk. Picking up a sheaf of papers, he sorted through them in a manner that made her heart sink. He seemed almost annoyed at her presence, and her mouth went dry at the way her heart suddenly ached.

"What can I do for you, Julia?"

The impersonal note in his voice made her wince. Had he actually given up on her? The question made her swallow a knot of fear in her throat. She had to stop thinking like this. If she wasn't careful, she'd be throwing herself into his arms.

Assuming a business-like manner, she rounded Morgan's large desk and laid the ledger she carried on the desktop in front of him. Immediately, a frisson slid over her skin as the warmth of his body heated hers simply by standing next to him. To her dismay, his entire body went rigid. It was as if the man found her presence detestable.

The thought squeezed at her heart, and she opened the ledger with an abrupt movement. When she found the appropriate page, she pointed to the account lines she'd been working on for most of the morning. Her finger pressed against the paper, she uttered a noise of frustration.

"These figures aren't adding up correctly."

Morgan didn't answer for a moment as he leaned over the book and trailed his finger over the numbers. Trembling, she pulled her hand away to avoid an accidental caress. Standing this close to him, she breathed in the warm spice scent of him. He smelled deliciously male.

Julia's heart skipped a beat as she watched his tapered finger tap restlessly against the ledger page. He had beautiful hands. They were strong and masculine. Her gaze focused on the light dusting of dark hair covering the back of his hand, and a familiar heat curled in her stomach the instant she remembered the way his hands had caressed her.

"Everything appears to be in order."

Jerked out of her reverie, she shook her head with frustration. "You don't understand, the Sea Witch was supposed to have a hundred more barrels of Madagascar oil than what she had when she arrived in port."

"That's because I had the captain stop at Gibraltar and hand over those barrels to the Bluebell for delivery to America."

"Oh." She frowned in puzzlement before turning to the Bluebell ledger page where the transaction had been noted. Feeling foolish, she shook her head. "I apologize."

"It was an efficient measure recommended by one of my investors." There was a slight trace of amusement in his voice.

The words took a moment to sink in before she realized she was the investor he'd referred too. Shortly after she'd purchased shares in St. Claire Shipping, she'd suggested he should consider using foreign ports-of-call as a means of transferring cargo more efficiently. The thought that he might actually listen to her suggestions had never crossed her mind.

Startled by the fact, Julia looked up at him. For the first time she realized how close they were to each other. The heat of him encircled her, while her heart crashed into her chest at a frantic pace. She missed his touch, and standing so close to him created the pulsating need to reach out and touch him. It took every ounce of willpower Julia possessed to keep from pressing her hand against his chest to see if his heart was racing with excitement like hers.

Hunger burned in his eyes as he watched her. It was a look that devoured her with an intensity that filled her with a longing she wanted to give way to. The muscle in his jaw flexed and the tension in him was almost palpable. If she were to touch him, his body would be hard as a rock. Would he be hard everywhere? The erotic thought shocked her, and her breathing immediately became shallower.

It was a scandalous thought, but it surprised her how much the idea excited her. Julia had never thought it possible that a man could make her feel desire as Morgan had done from the first moment they'd met. And as shocking as it was to think it, Julia wanted him to be hard with desire for her.

Beneath his piercing gaze, her insides melted, and Julia swayed into him. Morgan didn't look away, and elation sailed through her as she saw his head start to descend toward her mouth. He was going to kiss her. She shuddered at the desire speeding its way through her. Julia wanted him to kiss her until she couldn't think. It had been so long since the last time she'd been in his arms. Her eyes fluttered shut as she tipped her head back and eagerly awaited his lips to sear hers. When the heat of his body left her, her eyes flew open to see him watching her from several feet away.

"Is there anything else?"

The formality in Morgan's voice made her suppress a cry of frustration. Why was he addressing her with such polite civility? He'd held nothing back at other times, and especially not while they'd been in the throes of passion. Then he'd done everything he could to arouse her to a frenzied state.

An internal voice mocked her question. He was treating her exactly as she'd told him too. Even more disquieting was the knowledge that Julia didn't want him to listen to her. She wanted him to be masterful and commanding. She wanted him to kiss her senseless. Disconcerted by her thoughts, Julia swallowed hard as she realized she didn't want to leave Morgan's office. She searched her mind for the first excuse she could think of that would allow her to remain in the room.

"I noticed you've been out of the office several days this week. Did you have another migraine attack?"

"No. And while your concern is touching, it's unnecessary," he said tersely without giving her a reason for his absence.

This was not going well at all. Nibbling at her lip, she sent him a wary look. "I saw Colonel Beresford the other day. He mentioned he was hosting a dinner party for you and your investors, but I've not received my invitation."

"I told Beresford not to invite you."

His curt response sliced through her as she watched him stride back to the window and look out at the docks. Not invited. He'd deliberately had her excluded from a dinner party where business would most likely be discussed. Irritated, she glared at his back.

"So because I was the one to end…our liaison, you feel it necessary to bar me from business meetings."

"I do *not* base my business decisions on my personal affairs, Julia. You were not invited simply because attending the dinner would compromise you."

"I don't understand."

"It's more than likely you'd find the dinner party unsavory when it comes to some of the other guests

Beresford invited." He kept his gaze focused on the busy docks outside his window as if bored with the conversation.

"You mean there will be women there who are…who specialize in entertaining men."

"Exactly, which is precisely *why* I told Beresford he wasn't to invite you."

The icy emphasis on each of his words was almost a physical blow. Jealousy bit into Julia with the force of a wild animal at the thought of Morgan with another woman. Was he really trying to spare her or was it a way to control her? She quickly crossed the floor to his side, and with one hand, she forced him to face her.

"You can't do this," she said angrily. "This prevents Lady Falkenhouse and me from being privy to any business conducted at the dinner."

"Actually, you're the only investor who wasn't invited. Although Lady Falkenhouse *has* offered her regrets."

"So you gave her ladyship the choice to refuse attending, but not me," she snapped with outrage. "I never gave you permission to speak for me."

"In matters such as these I can, and *will*, speak for you, Julia." His response made her gasp with anger.

"You don't control me, Morgan St. Claire." She sent him a contemptuous glare. "I should have *known* that after one night in your bed you would consider me yours to command."

In a lightening move, Morgan jerked her into his arms. Startled by the action, she froze as tension drew her muscles up taut before the warmth of his body seeped into hers. Without thinking, she allowed herself to sink into him as desire wrapped its pleasurable sensation around her limbs.

This was what she'd been craving since she'd entered his office. His mouth brushed past her forehead, almost as if he were breathing in the scent of her hair. In the next instant, his lips were pressed against her ear lobe.

"Hear me, and hear me well, Julia. When it comes to protecting you from the advances of men like Beresford, I'll speak for you whenever I want. Do we understand each other?" There was an edge to his voice she'd not heard before.

"I don't need your protection," she said as she tried to push her way out of his arms. A pointless effort.

"What you need is protection from yourself," he said fiercely. "Beresford only mentioned the dinner in the hope you'd stubbornly insist on attending even though I'd informed him otherwise. The man's interest in you is blatantly obvious."

"Don't be absurd."

While it was true she found the Colonel's effusive compliments uncomfortable whenever she saw him, she'd never thought that the man might be interested in furthering his acquaintance with her.

"It's not a laughing matter." Morgan glared down at her. "The only reason the man's not called on you is because I made it clear to him some time ago that he's to stay away from you. His interest in you has *nothing* to do with St. Claire shipping. "

There was a possessive note in his voice that sent a tremor through her. Dark emotion glittered in his eyes, and she wasn't sure whether to be irritated by his masterful behavior or take pleasure in the fact that he wasn't about to let anything unpleasant happen to her. Something in his expression made her decide against being irritated. He had the look of a man determined to protect her at any cost.

Instinct guided her hand upward to brush her fingertips over his firm mouth. The sharp hiss of his breath against her skin sent a small thrill skimming down her back. Her gaze locked with his, and the hunger in his eyes stole her breath away. A fraction of a second later, and the emotion died a quick death. With a slight jerk, he released her and strode back to his desk. His departure left her vulnerable to the full impact of losing his warmth against her body.

"I've work to do, Julia." He picked up the ledger she'd brought into the office and offered it to her. "I believe this is yours."

Disappointment held her rigid as she stared at the green book and its red leather binding he held out to her. Last week he'd said he would give her time, but just now when she'd reached out to him, he'd pushed her away. An odd sensation spread its way into every inch of her, and it took her a moment to recognize it as sexual frustration.

What more did she have to do to make the man realize she wanted him. And she did. She wanted him with an intensity that shook her to the very core. One emotion after another assaulted her until she was on the verge of throwing herself at his feet and pleading with him to take her back into his bed.

Frightened that he could arouse her to such a piteous state, she darted forward and snatched the ledger from his hand. Whirling away from Morgan, she marched toward the door only to pause as he cleared his throat. Her hand on the brass doorknob, she turned her head to look at him. Morgan's expression was unreadable as he studied her.

"The next time you want to be kissed, Julia, don't expect me to read your mind," he said in a resolute tone of voice. "Ask."

He *had* known she wanted him, but he expected her to beg for his touch. He wanted her complete surrender. For the briefest of moments, she considered doing exactly that before she pulled herself back from the edge of insanity. Furious that she'd even contemplated giving in to his demand, she glared at him.

"And the next time you want to kiss *me*, Morgan St. Claire, *you'll* be the one begging to do so." Triumph made her tilt her head at a haughty angle as she saw surprise cross his face. Unwilling to give him a chance to respond, she tugged the door open and slammed it closed behind her. For a moment, she stood outside his office, her heart pounding with a mixture of fear and excitement.

Once again, she'd stood her ground with Morgan, and a small piece of her that Oscar had tried to destroy bloomed to life. It felt wonderful. Even if she couldn't allow herself to give in to her feelings for Morgan, their brief liaison had bolstered her confidence in a way she'd never imagined. A loud oath echoed through the door behind her, and like a mouse avoiding a trap, she hurried back to her small office. It was unlikely she'd be able to defy him again so soon after their most recent exchange. She needed time to gather her courage. If she were to face him now, she was quite apt to give way. And doing that would mean her heart wouldn't be the only thing lost to her. She would lose her soul as well.

Chapter 18

"Fuck," Morgan snarled.

Slowly sinking down into his large office chair, he reclined back against the leather padding, and closed his eyes. One hand rubbing the side of his head, he fought to control the familiar pangs of another headache.

Damn Beresford! If the man hadn't been his biggest investor, Morgan would have refused to attend the dinner the Colonel was arranging. The bastard had been trying for months to have a larger say in the running of St. Claire Shipping, and this was one more attempt to back Morgan into a corner. Unfortunately, it would be another year before he'd be in a financial position to buy the man out. But the day was coming, and Morgan looked forward to it. He groaned.

He should have known Julia would question him about the dinner. If he'd been thinking straight where she was concerned, he would have told her about Beresford and the party as soon as the Colonel had mentioned it was in the works. Instead, he'd done the one thing he should never have done with her. He'd taken away her ability to make her own decision.

In speaking for Julia, he'd put her on the defensive. It had been a foolhardy thing to do, but there wasn't a chance in hell that he'd let her attend that party. God knew what might have happened if the Colonel hadn't mentioned he'd invited several of Madame Evelyn's most popular ladies to attend the dinner. Beresford had been more than open about his interest in Julia, and despite his warnings, the Colonel clearly remained undaunted. And the way things stood between him and Julia, Morgan had no doubt Beresford would try and find a way to take advantage of the situation.

Morgan heaved a sigh at the thought. It had been evident that Julia hadn't even suspected that Beresford was interested in her. Her expression had made that quite clear. If he'd handled things differently, Beresford wouldn't be a problem at all where Julia was concerned. But it was a problem, and despite his best efforts, he continued to make mistakes where she was concerned.

For the past week, it had been difficult as hell to keep his distance from her. With the exception of passing her in the office, he'd not seen her since the theater. And her presence in his office just now had pushed the reserves of his willpower to the edge. It was only by a miracle that he'd been able to walk away from her when she closed her eyes and literally begged him in silence to kiss her. His cock twisted angrily in his trousers as he uttered a quiet oath. God, he wanted her. Needed her. Loved her.

But none of that mattered if she didn't come to him freely and of her own accord. She had to choose to be with him if they were to be truly happy. Keeping his distance for the past week had been born out of self-preservation. That night at the Lyceum, he'd wanted to carry her out of the theater despite her protests. Held in the grip of such powerful emotions, he knew he needed to stay away from her to prevent himself from doing something rash.

He'd never even considered the idea that his avoidance of her might encourage her to come to him of her own free will. But it seemed to have had the desired effect. It was the only explanation for her behavior a few moments ago. She was only just beginning to realize she wanted him. The question was whether she'd act on that impulse. Her behavior suggested she might, but if she didn't do it soon, he was going to go mad.

When he'd pulled her into his arms, she'd smelled delicious enough to devour. Pushing her away and acting nonchalant about doing so had been a supreme effort he wouldn't be able to repeat on a regular basis. He'd barely been able to resist her this time.

The woman had no idea what she'd done to him when she'd offered up her mouth for him to kiss. His entire body had been in agony as he'd walked away from her tempting offer. He'd been ready to take her here in his office, in broad daylight, where anyone could have interrupted them. Morgan groaned at the image knowing full well that as pleasurable as making love to her would be, he didn't just want her body. He wanted her love. Moments ago, she'd demonstrated her desire for him, but did her feelings run deeper? For his sanity, he had to believe they did. Anything less, would put him in a permanent state of hell.

Morgan walked from the entryway of the town house into the empty parlor. The fireplace was cold and empty, but it was easy to see how it would warm the room when there was a fire burning merrily in the hearth. More importantly, the room itself was bright and airy. He moved across the floor into the hallway.

"You'll find the house reasonably priced, Mr. St. Claire, it's a veritable bargain. The last owner outgrew the place, but there are plenty of bedrooms and a nursery as well. Not to mention the servants quarters on the third floor."

The solicitor gestured toward the flight of stairs leading to the second floor. Morgan nodded and climbed the steps with the man following him. The master bedroom was quite large, and he was pleased to find a sizeable dressing room adjoining it. Small and dimly lit, the room would make an excellent place for him to retreat during a migraine attack.

Leaving the bedroom, he took his time viewing the rest of the floor. The last room he came to was the nursery. Warm and cozy, it spoke of a childhood he had always wished for, but had never known. The happy ambiance to the room was in direct opposition to what he remembered of his childhood. He turned to the man waiting at the door.

"Draw up the papers for the sale and send them to me at the Clarendon. I'd like to take ownership by the end of the week."

"Certainly, sir. And will you require assistance securing furniture?"

"Yes, but only the necessities for the time being." He glanced around the nursery. He wanted Julia to have the pleasure of decorating the house. It would be one more way of showing her how much her happiness meant to him, and that he had no wish to crush her spirit or her sense of self.

Satisfied with his purchase, he left the house and strode down the steps to his carriage. Instructing his driver to return to the office, he climbed into the vehicle and settled back in the leather seat. Despite his pleasure at having found the ideal house, it had been an unsettling experience. Never having had the responsibility of a household, the notion of a permanent residence had proven more disturbing than he'd expected. Now that it was a *fait accompli*, he acknowledged the process had been a cleansing in some respects.

While it wasn't a home yet, it was a start. All that was required now was to convince Julia that his reasons for refusing Beresford on her behalf had been solely to protect her. Making her believe his intentions were well meant would be easy compared to the challenge of convincing her to marry him.

Her resistance to the idea wouldn't be easy to overcome. And after the incident in his office yesterday, he wasn't certain what to expect when he saw her next. The carriage rocked to a halt, and he stepped out of the vehicle. He'd taken two steps forward when, a firm hand settled on his shoulder.

"St. Claire." The simple greeting made Morgan turn his head then smile with pleasure at the sight of the man facing him.

"*Devlyn*. What the devil are you doing here?"

"Looking for you," the other man said as he shook Morgan's hand warmly. "I've an investment opportunity I thought might interest you."

"If it's one of your ideas, I'm certain it'll be quite profitable. That deal we brokered in America almost ten years ago is *still* generating a sizeable revenue."

Morgan opened the door to St. Claire Shipping's main building and ushered his friend into the quiet hum of his business. Once they entered his private office, Morgan gestured to one of the chairs in front of his desk before seating himself behind the large piece of furniture to study the man opposite him.

"Marriage agrees with you."

A grin of satisfaction on his face, Devlyn nodded. "Quite. Sophie is the best thing that ever happened to me."

"And where is the Countess?" Morgan reached out and offered his friend a cigar from the rosewood humidor on his desk.

"Thank you, no." Devlyn dismissed the tobacco with a wave of his hand. "Actually, Sophie and the children are getting settled in our new home over on Curzon Street. It's actually the first reason why I called on you. We want you to come for dinner Friday evening."

"I wouldn't miss it. What time—" A quiet knock made him send Devlyn an apologetic glance. "Come in."

The moment Julia entered the room Morgan's body tensed with the now familiar sensation of need that gripped him whenever she was near. It reflected a depth of emotion he'd never experienced until he'd met her. Until Julia had entered his life, Morgan had never understood what other men saw in the state of matrimony. He'd certainly never thought *he'd* be so eager to enter into such an arrangement. The permanency and restrictive nature of marriage had made him determined never to succumb to the idea, but Julia had persuaded him otherwise.

"Morgan, I wish to speak with you about this business dinner. I think—"

"I'm afraid it will have to wait, Julia," he said smoothly. She opened her mouth to argue then stopped as Devlyn rose to his feet.

"I'm sorry. I didn't realize you were busy. I can come back at a later time."

"Allow me to introduce my friend, the Earl of Devlyn. Devlyn, this is Mrs. Westgard."

Morgan watched in silence as she extended her hand to Devlyn. No one else watching her would ever have noticed the fine line of tension in her body. He'd always thought it part of her reserved manner, but he understood differently now. As Devlyn brushed his mouth over Julia's fingertips, a knot of unpleasant jealousy twisted his insides as the charm in his friend's smile. If Morgan hadn't known Devlyn was madly in love with his wife, he'd be stepping forward to put himself in front of Julia.

"Your husband is a fortunate man, Mrs. Westgard."

Delyn's words made Julia stiffen, and she immediately retreated behind that now familiar cool and distant façade she wore when feeling threatened. All too aware of her discomfort, Morgan cleared his throat.

"Julia is a widow, Devlyn." His friend turned his head to eye Morgan with surprise, and his jaw locked with tension under his friend's assessing gaze. "She's also one of my investors."

"Indeed." The one word echoed with a dozen unasked questions, and Devlyn turned back to Julia. "Tell me Mrs. Westgard, what the devil possessed you to invest in this notorious rake's company?"

"At the moment, I'm not exactly sure." Julia shot Morgan a glance of exasperation. "If I'd know precisely how autocratic the man could be, I think I would have thought twice about buying an interest in St. Clair Shipping."

Her words made Devlyn laugh loudly. The unexpected sound reverberated in the office, and Morgan saw Julia start with surprise. Devlyn shook his head as he eyed Morgan with great amusement.

"Is it possible there's one woman in the world that *hasn't* fallen under your spell, Morgan?" his friend joked.

"Julia's irritated with me because I refused an invitation on her behalf."

"I see," Devlyn sent Morgan a look of incredulity. "Sophie would have my head if I tried to do that."

"Beresford was the one extending the invitation." Morgan clasped his hands behind his back and experienced a surge of satisfaction as Delyn's face darkened with disgust. At least one person in the room thought his actions were justified.

"That reprobate?" Devlyn turned back to Julia. "Although it may have been presumptuous on St. Claire's part Mrs. Westgard, he made the right decision. Beresford is an utter cad."

"So my cousin told me at supper last night." Julia turned toward Morgan to offer him a hesitant smile. "I thought I would take her advice and express my regret at having doubted Morgan's intentions."

An apology. Morgan stared at her in amazement. A slight tinge of pink flooded her cheeks as she met his gaze. The contrite look on her lovely face made him want to pull her into his arms and kiss for having been so courageous. He was certain it had cost her a great deal to do apologize to him. Julia quickly averted her gaze from him and turned her attention back to Devlyn.

"Since I've done what I came to do, I'll leave the two of you to continue your discussion." She shot a brief glance toward Morgan and nodded at Devlyn before she moved quickly to the office door. Morgan started to go after her, but his friend moved faster.

"Mrs. Westgard, a moment if you please." Devlyn took her hand in his. "I wonder if you might do me a favor."

"A favor?" Although she hid it well, there was cool suspicion in her voice. Devlyn seemed oblivious to it, but Morgan heard crackling as she surrounded herself with an icy layer of reserve.

"You see, my wife doesn't have many friends in London, and I think you and she would get along quite well." The smile Devlyn sent her made Morgan's stomach clench as Julia smiled back, a distinct expression of relief flitting across her face.

"Oh…why of course. If you'll give me your address, I'd be happy to call on her."

"Actually, I was thinking perhaps you might join us for supper this Friday night. I know Sophie would be delighted to have you come."

"Supper? Oh, I—"

"Then you'll come." Devlyn paused as he waited for Julia to give way to his determination. When she reluctantly nodded, he smiled. "Excellent. Shall we say seven-thirty? We're at twelve Curzon Street."

The confusion on Julia's face made it clear she wasn't certain how she'd agreed to a dinner engagement. She looked adorable in her bewilderment, and Morgan bit back a smile as Devlyn kissed her hand then held the office door open for her. Julia hesitated for a brief moment as if she was going to say something then with a slight shake of her head she left the office.

As the door closed behind her, Devlyn turned around and grinned. "I believe you're expected at our house for dinner this Friday night as well."

Returning his friend's smile, he nodded his head. "I wouldn't miss it."

Chapter 19

The hackney cab rolled to a halt in front of twelve Curzon Street. Exiting the small carriage, Julia climbed the steps of the house and rapped on the door with the brass knocker.

A moment later, a short, elderly man opened the door and invited her inside. The man took her shawl and beaded bag from her just as a toddler charged across the hall with a loud laugh. A woman followed him at half a run.

"Master Spencer Blackwell, come back here this instant." Although her words were stern, there was the distinct sound of laughter in the woman's voice. With a quick maneuver, the woman caught up with the boy and scooped him up into her arms. Giggling with enthusiasm, the boy squirmed in his mother's arms as she pecked his cheek in a quick kiss and ordered him to be still.

As if suddenly realizing there was a guest in her foyer the woman turned to face Julia. A frazzled smile wreathing her handsome features, she sent the butler a beseeching look. "I'm terribly sorry. Fischer, would you mind taking Spencer up to Nanny? I'll take care of Mrs. Westgard."

The butler nodded and smiled as he took the boy into his arms and headed up the stairway. Their conversation was indiscernible, but it was obvious the boy adored the older man from the way the youngster laid his head on the butler's shoulder. Turning toward her, the woman smiled and stretched out her hand to Julia.

"Please forgive me. It *is* Mrs. Westgard, isn't it?"

Julia nodded as the woman shook her hand then drew her into a large salon. "I'm afraid perhaps I'm a little early, Lady Devlyn."

"No, you're right on time. And please, we're quite informal here. Do call me Sophie." The pleasant expression on Lady Devlyn's face drew her to Julia, and returning the woman's smile she nodded.

"All right, but I must insist you call me Julia."

"Julia. What a lovely name."

"I quite agree."

The deep, velvety sound of Morgan's voice made Julia go rigid. Slowly she turned her head and met his enigmatic gaze. Why the sight of him was so unexpected, she really didn't know. She should have known he would be here for supper since he and Lord Devlyn were friends.

"St. Claire."

With a nod in his direction, she managed to keep her voice steady as she greeted him, barely noticing that Lord Devlyn had entered the salon behind Morgan. Tension and heat tightened the muscles below her belly as she studied him for a brief moment before looking away. Just looking at the man was a dangerous pastime. Worse, she found it was impossible to remain unaffected by the raw force of his personality even from across the room.

Every time she saw him, her need for him slowly eroded the slippery slope she stood on. Soon, she'd have to make a decision where he was concerned. Not only did she want his kiss and touch, she wanted one more chance to experience the ecstasy of that single night they'd spent in each other's arms. The knowledge didn't really surprise her, but the intensity of her craving for him did. Determined not to reveal how vulnerable she was to his presence, she turned back to Lady Devlyn.

"My la—" She stopped at the pleasant look of discouragement on Sophie's face and smiled. "Sophie. How old is your little boy?"

"Spencer will be four in about six months, although he seems far older than that sometimes."

A deep laugh poured out of Lord Devlyn's throat as he moved to his wife's side. Pressing a kiss to her cheek, he grinned. "He's his mother's son—impudent and well aware that he has the entire staff wrapped around his finger."

"Supper will be ready shortly, but until then please make yourselves comfortable." With a gesture toward the couches separated by an oval coffee table, Sophie sank down onto one of the sofas. Julia followed suit and sat down across from her hostess. An instant later, her skin grew hot as Morgan joined her on the love seat. Inhaling a deep breath, she trembled at how close he was.

Perched on the edge of her seat, her mouth tightened with annoyance as she heard his low chuckle. Determined to ignore him, she watched Lord Devlyn take his wife's hand and hold it in his in a tender gesture. They were the image of a happily married couple. A streak of envy flashed through her. Quickly she killed the emotion. Marriage was out of the question for her. Leaning forward slightly, she smiled.

"Lord Devlyn tells me you've only recently moved into this house."

"Yes, it's been a little more than two months now. We haven't been frequent visitors to town, but with this new venture Quentin is starting, we needed a place to stay and entertain."

Devlyn leaned toward his wife with a wicked grin. "Admit it, my love, you simply want to drag me to the blasted opera. Although, I confess there is one opera I have quite pleasurable memories of."

A delicate blush crept over Sophie's cheeks, and once more, Julia found herself envying the affectionate rapport between the couple. Is this what the words happily married meant? This give and take between a husband and wife. She darted a glance at the man beside her. Morgan's eyes met hers in a quiet look of assessment. The sudden hunger darkening his gaze sent a shudder of longing through her.

Had he arranged this supper invitation in his efforts to persuade her to marry him? If he had, he'd wasted his time. Still, she couldn't help wondering what life would be like if she were to marry him? The thought made her tug her gaze away from him as she struggled to cope with the sharp desire to consider his proposal. A small chill streaked across her skin at how strong the urge to give in to him was.

From the salon doorway, a young maid announced dinner, and Julia allowed a soft sigh of relief to part her lips as she quickly stood up. Seconds later, her relief vanished as Morgan rose to his feet to stand next to her. A wave of heat washed over her skin at his close proximity, while her heart pounded wildly in her chest. She offered up a small prayer that they weren't alone. If they had been, she was certain she would have done exactly as he'd told her the other day. She would have asked him to kiss her. Julia trembled slightly and glanced up at Morgan. His eyes narrowed as if he could read her mind, and her mouth went dry as she met his gaze. Resisting temptation was proving to be far more difficult than she'd ever thought possible.

Ever since Julia had learned Morgan had arranged to take her home after supper, her body had been stiff with irritation. The pleasant manner with which she'd said goodbye to Devlyn and Sophie was in direct contrast to the frosty silence in the carriage. She'd even refused his hand climbing into his carriage.

The interior of the vehicle created an intimacy he liked, but it was clear Julia didn't feel the same way. She'd twisted her body away from him so the only thing brushing against his legs was the taffeta of her green silk dress. The carriage rocked forward, and the only sound inside the vehicle was that of the horse's hooves against the cobblestone street.

Julia stared out the window in silence, and it was impossible to imagine what she might be thinking. The tension between them could have been kindling it was so brittle, and he was certain of one thing. She was far from happy with him at the moment. He released a quiet sigh of frustration. Somehow, he had to convince her that marriage wasn't a prison, but a chance for immeasurable happiness.

His friends' happy marriage was the perfect example of what he was certain he and Julia could have. Until just recently, he'd always thought Devlyn's and Sophie's happiness was something to envy. He'd never dreamed such happiness might be within his grasp until he met Julia.

All evening, he'd watched her studying the other couple when she thought no one was watching, and it had given him hope that she'd been thinking they could be just as happy together as Sophie and Devlyn. Studying her profile, he cleared his throat.

"Did you enjoy yourself this evening?"

"Yes." She didn't look at him as she spoke. "I like Sophie a great deal."

"I could tell she liked you as well." When she didn't respond, his jaw muscles tightened with frustration. Stubborn as always, she refused to make things easy between them.

"Their marriage is a happy one. I've always thought them well suited for one another." At his comment, she slowly turned to look him in the eye.

"They *are* well suited, unlike *others*."

"If by that you think we're ill-suited for one another then you're wrong. We belong together. You're just too obstinate to see it." He folded his arms across his chest to keep from reaching out and shaking her.

"And you're *not* stubborn?" She sniffed with heated sarcasm. "You continue to tout this idea that marriage is a suitable state for the two of us, when I know it would be anything but."

"Tell me *why* you think that."

"Because…because if I marry you, the law gives you complete control over me," she snapped. "And I refuse to let that happen."

"If it's your money you're worried about, I'm perfectly willing to sign a document that prevents me for having access to any of your finances." He saw her jerk at his statement before she shook her head and looked out the window.

"My finances are not what I'm talking about," she said softly. "The moment I married you, I'd be nothing more than your property. An object you could do with as you like."

"*Christ Jesus*," he rasped. "I'm nothing like Westgard, Julia. Hurting you would be the last thing I'd ever want to do. I love you."

"And I…I know that."

The way she stumbled over her words made his heart crash violently into his chest. She'd almost admitted she loved him before she caught herself. He was certain of it. In a swift move, he reached out and pulled her into his lap. In the dim light, he saw her lips part in surprise.

"Say it, Julia. Tell me you love me." His harsh command made her shake her head in denial.

"You're wrong," she said breathlessly, her body rigid against his. "And even if you weren't, it wouldn't change my mind about marrying *you* or anyone else."

Morgan bowed his head to smell the soft fragrance of her skin. As much as he desired her, he was equally happy just being near her. No matter how old they grew, Morgan knew that would never change. She was as important to him as the air he breathed. But he also loved touching her, tasting her. He brushed his mouth across her bare shoulder.

The quick breath she dragged into her lungs pleased him. He enjoyed knowing that he had the same effect on her that she had on him.

Lifting his head, he covered her mouth with his in a passionate kiss while his hand cupped the back of her neck and pulled her tight against him. Beneath his caress, she grazed his lips with the tip of her tongue. The erotic touch pulled a deep groan from him, and a second later, he was tasting the inside of her mouth.

God, he wanted to shut out the world until she surrendered to him completely. The taste of sweet wine on her tongue blended with the peaches they'd had for dessert like a delicious nectar. His thumb found the pulse fluttering frantically at the side of her neck. It beat an erotic tattoo against the pad of his finger.

In his trousers, his erection jutted up toward his stomach with a needy throb. The soft mewl escaping her throat nearly undid him completely. Christ Jesus, but the woman had him wrapped around a barrel. She could ask him for anything at the moment and he'd give it to her.

Deepening their kiss, he struggled to keep from lifting her dress and stroking her with his fingers. There was no doubt she'd be wet with liquid heat. His cock jumped at the thought while his ballocks drew up tight against his groin. Damn, he didn't want her like this. He wanted her to come to him of her own choosing. But God help him, he didn't think he had the strength to refuse what she was willing to give him right now.

His hands slid across her bare skin to where her gown hugged the edge of her shoulder. Beneath his touch, she trembled. Her tongue danced with his for a moment longer before she broke away from his kiss. Agitation marked her movements as she hastily unbuttoned his shirt and pulled it out of his trousers with a sharp tug.

The moment her hands touched the hot flesh of his chest, the desire building inside her belly rushed to the apex of her thighs in a taut explosion of fiery need. Eager to taste him, she pressed her mouth to his hard torso. Muscles rippled against her lips as he leaned back into the carriage's leather cushions with a quiet groan.

The sound gave her a sense of power, and she loved knowing how much her touch pleased him. Slowly and methodically, she brushed his skin with kisses until her tongue flicked out to circle his nipple. Another low rumble echoed in his chest, the vibration teasing her lips as she savored the tangy taste of him.

Sweet heaven, she'd missed him. Missed this. It had been too long since she'd been in his arms. And she needed him. Wanted him inside her, filling her, throbbing against her tautness until they both caught fire and exploded at the same instant. Her senses swimming with heat and need, she nipped at the side of his neck with her teeth as her hand slid down to stroke the hard length of him pressing into her thigh.

He jumped as her touch. Through the material of his trousers, he was hot and harder than she remembered. He wanted her. Jubilant at the knowledge, she applied a gentle pressure to him, and he groaned deeply. Tonight, she was willing to give in to her passion. Tomorrow, she'd face the consequences of her actions.

Strong fingers captured her chin, and he took her mouth again in a mind-searing kiss. Lost to the sensations flooding her senses, her fingers spiked through his hair as she returned his kiss with all the passion exploding inside her. A warm hand stroked her bare throat down to the valley between her breasts.

A shudder sped through her as his hand cupped her. Her rigid nipples scraped with agonizing sensitivity against her undergarments at the touch. Whimpering with the need for more, her fingers sought the buttons of his trousers as her hunger for him spiraled out of control. Desire flooded her body and touching him was all that mattered.

With a suddenness that jerked her out of her aroused state, Morgan's large hands encircled her waist like a vise and returned her to the seat opposite him. Her breathing ragged, she looked into his eyes in bewilderment. What was wrong with him? He'd provoked this intense encounter. Why had he pushed her away? The dark hunger in his eyes made her reach out to touch his cheek. He caught her wrist and pushed her hand aside with a harsh shake of his head.

"Not like this, Julia," he rasped as he buttoned his shirt in an unsteady fashion.

"I...I don't understand." Bemused by his abrupt rejection, she shook her head. "You kissed me. I...thought you..."

"I do want you, Julia. I want you more than you know." Shoving his shirt back into his trousers, he grimaced. "But you have to come to me of your own free will."

"I just offered myself to you, and you reject me simply to demand that I come to *you*," she said fiercely.

"You didn't offer, Julia. You gave into desire." His voice was implacable as he watched her with his narrowed gaze.

"I can assure you, St. Claire, if I had *not* wanted to be seduced, you would not have found me so willing," she bit out through clenched teeth.

"And that's the problem Julia. I want you to be with me by choice, not because I seduced you." The sigh he released was one of great weariness, and her heart slammed against her chest at the sound. "If you care for me, you'll come to me at a time of your choosing. Completely free of any enticement from me."

"What you mean is that I have to bow to your will and beg you to take me into your bed."

"No. I'm asking for more than that. I know how important your independence is to you, but I want to know you're going to be there when I come home at night."

"But you don't have a home—you have rooms in a hotel," she said with a sniff of derision.

"Not any longer. I've bought a house. A house that needs a woman's touch. I want that woman to be you."

The words echoed like gunfire inside the carriage. She wasn't quite certain she'd heard him correctly, and yet she knew she had. For a long moment, she simply absorbed his news. He'd bought a house. Morgan St. Claire—confirmed bachelor, unmitigated womanizer—had bought a house.

He was up to something. She didn't know what, but he was scheming to get his own way. First, he'd proposed marriage and now a house. There had to be some ulterior motive for his behavior. What did he want? Meeting his dark gaze from across the carriage, a tremor went through her. The open hunger and longing in his eyes did more than confuse her. It frightened her.

Dear God, could the man possibly be telling her the truth. The carriage rolled to a stop. In silence, they exited the vehicle and Morgan escorted her up the three steps to her front door. As her hand grasped the doorknob, a large hand covered hers.

"We'll not see each other again unless you choose to be with me, Julia." There was a grim tilt to his mouth. "Come to me. Don't let that bastard you married win."

Without waiting for a response, he left her standing on the front stoop and returned to his carriage. The finality in his voice made her throat close in fear. Would he really not see her again? Something told her this might be the last time she ever saw him. Inside a voice cried out for her to run after him, but she crushed the protest. No. She couldn't agree to his terms. She would have to live without Morgan St. Claire. No matter how painful and difficult that would be.

Chapter 20

ulia passed through the main door of St. Claire Shipping, her gaze automatically flitting toward Morgan's office door. Just as it had been for the past two weeks, the door stood open. It was a declaration that Morgan had not yet arrived.

Worrying her lip with her teeth, she walked slowly toward the small office she used. There was little need for her to even be here today. She'd finished reviewing all of Morgan's accounting ledgers days ago, and there wasn't much else for her to review. If she were honest with herself, the only reason she was in the shipping office was because she wanted to see Morgan.

She'd not seen him since the night he'd left her standing at her front door. When he'd left her, there had been such a finality in his demeanor. It had only been in the last week that she'd begun to realize that he'd been quite serious about not seeing her again. Her hand grasped the cool brass of the office doorknob, but she didn't turn it. She stood there for a moment as if suspended in time.

Morgan was a good businessman. Surely, he wouldn't stay away from the office for such a long time simply because he wanted to avoid her. Even if he were ill, she would have seen him here in the office. What if he had gone out of town on business? That would make sense. She whirled around and walked over to Morgan's head clerk, Jeremy Crane.

"Mr. Crane, I was wondering if you could tell me where Mr. St. Claire is?"

"I'm not certain, Mrs. Westgard." The clerk shook his head.

"Have you heard from him at all?"

"It seems he's been working mostly at night, madam," the clerk said with a slight frown. "He's generally here when I arrive in the morning and leaves a short time afterward. Although I've not seen him for the past three mornings."

"Working nights," she gasped softly. He *was* avoiding her.

"He's always kept odd hours, madam. Although, he didn't look all that well the last time I saw him." The man's response made her stomach lurch. Had Morgan made himself unwell working through the night?

"When did you see him last?"

"Three days ago. He instructed me to send any paperwork needing his attention to this address until he returned."

The clerk reached for a slip of paper resting on his desk and handed it to her. Morgan's strong, elegant penmanship filled the sheet, and she stared at the address for a long moment. A desperate longing clutched at her heart. She needed to know he was all right. She trembled as she handed the paper back to the head shipping clerk.

"Thank you, Mr. Crane. If by chance Mr. St. Claire does come into the office today, would you please let him know that I'd like to speak with him?"

"Of course, Mrs. Westgard, of course."

Nodding her head toward the clerk, she walked out of Morgan's shipping office. The address Crane had shown her rolled about in her head. It was in the fashionable residential district. Could this be the house Morgan had bought? Had he simply been working at home for the past three days in an effort to avoid her or had he taken ill as Crane seemed to think?

She signaled for her carriage and gave her driver Morgan's address before settling herself in the vehicle. It was most likely the worst mistake she could make, but she had to know he was all right. Her head resting against the soft leather padding she stared out the window as the carriage rolled forward.

She should call out and tell Dobson to take her home. It would be the sane thing to do. Whether Morgan had been ill or not, her sudden appearance on his doorstep would have the man thinking she'd finally decided to come to him of her own free will. Julia winced. It was true, she was coming of her own accord, but it was merely to ensure Morgan was well. The lie made her throat swell shut.

Over the past two weeks, she'd been trying to convince herself it would be easy to live without Morgan. She'd thought it would be easy to crush the love she had for him. Not only had she been mistaken. She'd been miserable too. Miserable without the sound of his voice or the sight of his face to brighten her day. And the longer she went without seeing him, the more she realized how much pleasure she found in his company.

A sigh parted her lips. Morgan had allowed her to win one battle after another, but he'd won the war between them from the moment of that first kiss in his rooms at the Clarendon. The carriage rolled to a halt, and she leaned forward to look out the window. Morgan had warned her that she would have to come to him on her own. Now, she was doing just that.

The thought made her wince as she studied the lovely stone façade of the residence she saw through the carriage window. Larger than the usual town home, the dwelling was impressive and yet inviting at the same time. The house Morgan had purchased was much larger than she'd envisioned.

She exited the vehicle and quickly climbed the steps to ring the bell. A moment later, the door opened without a squeak to reveal Mrs. Welkin's pleasant countenance. Morgan had obviously convinced the hotel housekeeper to come manage his home. If he were ill, Mrs. Welkins knew exactly how to take care of him, and Julia had worried needlessly.

"Mrs. Westgard, how lovely to see you," The housekeeper opened the door wide. "Won't you come inside?"

Now that she was here, the uncertainty inside her grew. Morgan had no need of her if he was unwell. He would be well cared for by Mrs. Welkins. Then there was the scandalous nature of her visit. Although Julia wasn't a debutante in danger of sullying her reputation, it was still scandalous for her to be calling on a man. Particularly a man of Morgan's notoriety. It was the kind of behavior Oscar would have condemned with a malicious snub. The thought made Julia step impulsively into the large, empty foyer. As the housekeeper closed the front door, Mrs. Welkins gestured toward a closed door.

"Mr. St. Claire is in the study. I think he'll be pleased to see you. I know he thinks quite highly of you." Julia stiffened in surprise as she turned her head toward the older woman who smiled. "He's not said anything, but I recognize the signs of a man in love."

Heat filled Julia's cheeks at the woman's observation. Feeling more than a little uncomfortable, she hesitated. She ought to leave right now. Her brain immediately rejected the thought. Impossible. She didn't want to go another day, not even another hour, without seeing him. With a nod at the housekeeper, she moved through the door into the study. Candles, and a small fire in the hearth, lit the room, while heavy maroon curtains covered the windows and blocked out the sunshine.

"Come in and shut the door, whoever you are."

The deep harsh tone of Morgan's voice scraped across her senses as she quickly carried out his command. Her eyes slowly adjusted to the dim light as the door clicked closed behind her. It took her a few seconds to find Morgan. He was sitting in a large library chair a small distance from where she stood.

Long legs stretched out in front of him and crossed at the ankles, he was the epitome of dangerous male beauty. He wasn't wearing a jacket, and the white of his shirt was a sharp contrast to the deep wine leather of the chair. She took a step forward then stopped as Morgan's eyes slowly opened. The air crackled between them as she saw him jerk in surprise before he narrowed his gaze at her.

"What are you doing here, Julia?" His voice was flat and devoid of emotion.

Swallowing her nervousness, she searched his darkened features. There was just enough firelight to reveal his profile, but his eyes were unreadable in the shadows. A tremor shot through her.

"I came…I came because I thought you were ill."

"As you can see, I'm quite well." The words were staccato beats in the thick air of tension filling the room.

"If you're well, why do you have the drapes pulled and all the candles lit?"

"Mrs. Welkins knows being in the dark helps me recover more quickly from a migraine."

"So you have been unwell," she exclaimed as she took another step toward him.

"I'm quite recovered."

"I'm pleased to hear it," she said with an enormous sense of relief. Silence filled the room, and she struggled not to fidget.

"I've been waiting for you." There was a rough edge to his voice as he watched her from his seat. He didn't move, but she could see the strained tautness of his body. "I'd just about given up hope."

"I simply came to see if you were ill."

She grew still as he uncurled his large frame out of his chair and moved toward her. Unable to move, she shuddered the moment he closed the distance between them. He bent his head until his mouth brushed lightly against her ear.

"Liar."

The heat from his body was an inferno across her skin. Tilting her head back, she looked up into his eyes. They blaze with a hunger that pulled her muscles tight with anticipation. Julia swallowed hard as she tried to speak, but her throat was dry. She ached for him to touch her, but he didn't move. He was clearly waiting for her to reach out to him. Something pulsed between them, and she trembled at the desire building in her like a violin's crescendo.

"Tell me why you're really here, Julia," he rasped.

The words formed in her head, but it was too difficult to speak them, and she shook her head as her courage failed her. She bit down on her lip. Worry might have been the catalyst bringing her here, but she would have come even if she'd known he was hale and hearty. She was certain he knew why she was here. She'd come to him, just as he'd demanded.

"I've already told you. I wanted to ensure that you were in good health."

"Then now that you've seen I'm well, there's no need for you to stay," Morgan growled as he wheeled away from her and returned to his chair.

Startled by his reaction, she frowned. The man was impossible. Hadn't she done as he asked? She'd come to him, but she refused to beg for his touch. Frustrated, she clenched her hands and one balled fist burrowed its way through a thick layer of silk to press into her leg.

"Blast you St. Claire. I came as you asked—no— *demanded.* I came here not just because I was concerned about you, but because I wanted to. What more do you want from me?"

Silence filled the room, and she tried to read his expression as she glared at him. Why was she standing here, allowing him to control her like this? The question made her suck in a deep breath. No. He wasn't the one in control. She was. She could easily leave. All she had to do was walk away from him. But she didn't want to.

"I want you to undress for me." His soft words pierced her turbulent thoughts.

"Wha…What?"

"Remove your clothes. Slowly." This time it was a command, and she stiffened with fear at the idea of baring herself while he sat there watching her.

"You're mad," she snapped.

"Mrs. Welkins won't interrupt us."

"But…I…"

"Afraid?"

Despite the arrogant smile on his lips, there was a hint of fear in the way he leaned forward slightly in his chair. As if realizing how much his posture revealed, Morgan reclined back into the massive armchair and arched an eyebrow at her. Muscles tight and taut under his piercing gaze, she narrowed her eyes at him.

He'd regained control of his emotions, and yet she had no doubt that he wanted her. Although he appeared relaxed, desire flickered briefly in his eyes. It had been maddening to have him so close just a moment ago and know that she'd not been able to tempt him into losing control. And now— now he wanted her to undress for him while he watched.

Just once, she'd like to turn the tables on the man. Tease him. Tempt him. Drive him to distraction until he— her thoughts crashed to a halt. Morgan had always been the one pleasuring her. What if *she* pleasured him? The idea sent her heart slamming into her chest.

Could she be that daring? Was this what Morgan had been trying to show her all along? That she had the ability to direct the path their lovemaking took if she only had the courage to try. Fear cascaded through her. Whirling around, she hurried toward the door.

182

Chapter 21

The moment she turned away and raced for the door, Morgan was on his feet. He was out of his mind if he let her go. Christ Jesus, she'd come to him as he'd asked. All he had to do was take her into his arms, and she'd be his.

But he wanted more. He wanted her heart to lead her to him. The instant she wrapped her hand around the doorknob he took a step forward then froze as she hesitated.

For a long moment, she stared at the door handle until she slowly turned the key in the lock. The tension holding him rigid fled his body as Julia faced him. The hesitant look on her face required every bit of restraint he possessed not to stride across the room and pull her into his arms.

Morgan knew it hadn't been easy for her to come to him. Even if she'd done so under the pretense of her concern for him, he didn't care. She was here. A wave of uncertainty rolled over Morgan, and to harness the emotion, he sank down into his chair and waited. The look of confidence sweeping over her face made him stiffened. It was as if she'd recognized his indecision and had taken strength from it.

Julia walked forward until she was only a few feet away from him. For a brief moment, he saw her courage falter before a sultry confidence darkened her eyes. His cock stirred in his trousers at the sight of her. God, she was beautiful.

With slow, deliberate precision, her hand glided up from her waist to cup her breast then circle the silk over her nipple with her forefinger. His mouth had been dry for several minutes, but now he was parched. Mesmerized, he could only watch in mute fascination as she reached behind her to undo her dress. The movement sent her breasts jutting outward, and made him hard as iron.

There was an uninhibited air about her that amazed and excited him. He didn't know what had changed her mind, but he didn't care. The woman from the portrait met his gaze boldly and without shame. Had he finally won? Had he truly succeeded in making her realize that being with him was her choice?

Candlelight shimmered across Julia's face, giving her a luminescent quality. Enthralled, he sucked in a sharp breath as their gazes locked and she slipped her dress off one softly rounded shoulder. It made him crave the heat he knew resided between her thighs. Watching her like this made him hot. Hotter than he'd been the night she'd come to his bed.

She pushed the dress downward as she continued to disrobe. He'd thought himself hard already. But when her corset came off and the light mocha color of her nipples peeked through her thin chemise, his cock jumped in a silent demand for action. But he didn't move. He couldn't. It might break the spell she was casting on him. And he didn't want that to happen. Not yet.

Moments later she stood in front of him completely exposed. With a half smile curving her lips, she reached up to undo her hair. The movement lifted her breasts higher, and he ached to flick his tongue across her hard nipples. Silky, burnt sienna tresses tumbled down onto her shoulders and dipped to brush across the stiff peaks.

"Is this what you wanted me to do, Morgan?" The husky tone of her voice shot anticipation through him.

"Yes," he growled.

She moved toward him and knelt at his feet. He smelled the lemony scent of her hair. There was also the scent of her passion. It was a hot musk, and it teased his senses until he was rigid with longing. Not once did her gaze waver from his face as she rested her hand on his hard length.

The moment she did so, he sucked in a deep breath. God almighty, she was a siren. She'd bewitched him. He didn't move as her fingers undid his trousers. As his cock sprang out in eager anticipation of plunging into her heated depths, he struggled to control his ragged breathing. He failed the moment she reached out to touch him.

One elegant finger traced a line from the tip of him down to his ballocks. It was a light touch, but it generated an excruciating need for more. Seconds later, the warmth of her hand encircled him, and he released a groan of pleasure. Firelight threw one side of her face into the shadows, but the gleam in her hazel eyes warned him she knew *exactly* what she was doing.

It was a confidence he'd not seen in her before, but it was clear she knew how she was making him feel. Even more visible in her features was the way she was reveling in that knowledge. He watched her head descend toward his cock. Good god, was she—

"*Christ Jesus,*" he rasped as her tongue stroked up the length of him and swirled around the tip of his cock. The seductive caress made his erection expand further. Barely able to control his need, he slid his hands through the silk of her hair and jerked as she blew a hot, yet cool breeze across his bare skin. Her tongue slid over him once more before her beautiful mouth wrapped around him in a tight grip.

The flick of her tongue over the ridge of him tugged another groan from him, and he looked down to watch her mouth slide up and down his erection. It was the most erotic thing he'd ever witnessed. With each stroke, she increased the pace until the exquisite friction of her mouth on him sent his senses reeling. Barely able to think straight, he threaded his hands through her silky tresses and rocked his hips against her mouth.

He'd had the best suck on his cock, and not one of them had come close to making him ready to explode as quickly as she did. With each swirl of her tongue, she was driving him closer to the edge of a pleasure he'd never thought any woman could arouse in him. Suddenly, her mouth tightened around him like a hot vise then she tugged her head up and retreated from him.

Stunned, he jumped as her fingers brushed against his ballocks and cool air swept over his cock. His eyes flew open to watch her rise to her feet and stand in front of him, the reddish-brown curls at the apex of her thighs so close and yet so far away.

He struggled not to lose control of his faculties as she trailed her fingers over her breasts and caressed her nipples. In disbelief, he watched one hand trail down over her stomach to part her velvety folds and stroked herself.

"Do you enjoy watching me like this, Morgan?"

The husky sound of her voice tantalized him, while the sultry twist of her lips teased him as he watched her play with herself. His eyes caught a glimpse of cream on her fingers, and he groaned. It was time to end this tempting display and take what his body demanded. Christ, his body wasn't just demanding satisfaction it shouted for it. He reached out for her, but she took a quick step back, and a small smile curved her mouth as she trailed her fingers across her rigid nipples again.

The look of astonishment on his face pleased her. For once, she was in control, and she liked it. She hadn't expected to enjoy taking him into her mouth, but she had.

Even more pleasing was knowing she was responsible for his harsh breathing and growls of excitement.

It was a powerful sensation that had increased her confidence to the point that she felt no shame or embarrassment touching herself so boldly in front of him. She was certain this was what he'd meant when he'd said he wanted the bold woman in the portrait.

Cupping her breasts, she rolled her thumbs over the stiff peaks, her fingertips skating over her dimpled areoles. He didn't take his eyes off of her, and the desire in his expression thrilled her.

"You didn't answer me, Morgan, do you enjoy watching me play with myself?"

"*Yes, goddamnit.* It's one of the most erotic things I've ever seen in my life." His voice was hoarse as he rose to his feet and stepped toward her. She retreated again.

"Do you want me?" Heart pounding, she waited for his reply.

"Damn it, you know I do. I want you *now.*"

The growled response made her draw in a quick breath of anticipation as he stepped forward. She reached out her hand and pressed it against his chest, stopping him in his tracks. Beneath her hand, his heart beat a fast pace into the surface of her palm, while his breathing was ragged as if he'd run a great distance.

"How badly do you want me?" Her question made him narrow his eyes at her.

"What game are you playing at, Julia?"

"It's not a game. I simply need to know how badly you want me." She deliberately reached out to delve her hand into his open trousers and grasped him in a tight grip. "Tell me."

"God in heaven, woman, do you want me to beg?" he groaned.

"Would you?" She held her breath as she watched his jaw flex with tension.

"Yes," he rasped as he caught her shoulders in a rough grip. "I'd move heaven and earth for you. I'll give you anything you ask. Just let me love you."

Her hand slid off his erection and she pressed her body against him. The tip of his phallus pressed into her curls as she pulled his head down toward hers. Brushing her mouth against his, she laced her tongue over the seam of his lips.

"That's all I wanted to hear," she whispered.

The groan rumbling deep in his chest reverberated over her skin, and she melted into him welcoming his passionate kiss. Beneath her hands, the soft fabric of his shirt interfered with her need to touch him, and her fingers frantically undid the buttons as his tongue swept into her mouth.

Eager to feel his hard muscles beneath her hands, she tugged his shirt open and glided her fingertips across the hard ridges of his chest. A hot need uncurled in her belly and sped through her limbs until it consumed her. As he discarded his shirt in a rough movement, he pulled her closer, and her nipples tingled as they rubbed against his chest.

His mouth slanted off hers and blazed a path of heat down her throat to one breast. The moment the heat of his tongue swirled around her nipple, her legs wobbled beneath her. The masculine, spicy scent of him filled her senses as her body cried out for his possession. A moan parted her mouth as her fingertips dug into his shoulders in an effort to remain standing.

"Oh God, Morgan. I want you. I want to feel you inside me."

Lifting his head, his thumb continued to stroke the sharp peak of her breast. He shuddered against her, but there was a determined look in his eyes as he stared down at her.

"Say it, Julia." His words made her stiffen as he wrapped his arms tight around her to keep her from escaping him. "It's only three words, sweetheart."

"Morgan, please…" She swallowed hard as she shook her head. His expression tender, pleading almost, he pressed his forehead against hers. It undid her. "I…I love…you."

The moment she uttered the words, amazement crashed its way into every part of her. She'd done it. She'd actually admitted her feelings for him. It created a sense of freedom inside her. As he exhaled a deep breath, Julia realized he'd been unsure of her. The knowledge startled her.

He'd always presented such a sure and confident façade. To think that Morgan St. Claire, renowned womanizer, might be uncertain of her was astonishing. In the next moment, his hard kiss against her mouth drove all thought from her head, and every nerve ending in her body pulsed with a steady rhythm that cried out for completion.

Morgan pulled Julia down to the large Brussels carpet beneath their feet. The moment they reached the floor, he tore his way out of the rest of his clothing all too cognizant of her feverish kisses along the line of his jaw and down to the base of his throat. He released a harsh breath at the way her touch aroused not only his body, but his heart as well.

His hands cupped her face as he slid his tongue past her lips to explore the warmth of her mouth. She tasted like a delicious blend of sweet wine and fiery cognac. Their tongues mated in a hot duel of desire until his cock ached to be buried inside her heat.

Unable to wait any more, he fell backward to the floor, pulling her with him. Silky skin caressed the pads of his fingers as he grasped her round hips, then with a sharp tug he settled her slick velvet folds over his hardness. As her honeyed sweetness slid over him, he surged up into her with a guttural cry of pleasure.

Christ, she felt good wrapped around his cock. Her muscles clutched and squeezed him with intense pleasure. It would be fast this time, but there would be plenty of time later to indulge in each other. The spasms rippling over his hard length came fast and furious as she shuddered with each stroke. Arching her back, she pressed her hands into the top of his thighs meeting his thrusts with equal measure. She'd come to him, and after today, she would always be his. As she rode him at a frantic pace, a familiar tightening grabbed at his groin, and as he thrust his body against hers one last time, he uttered a low cry as his cock throbbed hard inside her

Her release quickly followed his, and she shuddered violently over him before falling forward. For several long moments, they didn't move as the tremors cascading through her subsided. Spent from the intensity of their lovemaking, he pulled her close against him, nestling her against his chest. He'd never known such contentment as this, and it was all her doing. His life and happiness rested in her hands.

The keen emotions coursing through Julia's veins frightened her. All the what ifs held the last small vestiges of her heart hostage. Yet despite her fears, she was convinced she belonged in Morgan's arms. Warm lips pressed against her forehead as a soft laugh rumbled out of him.

"You continue to amaze me, sweetheart. I always knew you had a bold streak in you, but you've surpassed anything I'd imagined." The tenderness in his voice tugged at Julia's heart. Raising herself up to hover over him, she smiled.

"Does that mean you like it when I'm naughty?" she teased. Morgan laughed and nodded.

"Absolutely. And when we're married, I'll teach you how to be naughtier still."

His words laced her muscles with tension, and with a quick movement, she pulled away from him and climbed to her feet. Marriage. The dragon reared its terrifying head. How could she make him understand how willing she was to be his mistress? Eager in fact. But marriage? It was out of the question. Without looking at him, she found her undergarments and began to dress.

"Out with it, Julia. Tell me what's going on in that complex brain of yours."

With a glance over her shoulder, she saw him sit up and arch his brow at her. One leg bent, his arm rested on top of his knee. She'd never seen a more resplendent picture of male beauty. Strong, muscular, and seductive, he stole her breath away. His gaze narrowed when she didn't answer. Scrambling to his feet, he caught her arm and turned her to face him.

"Something's wrong."

"No. Not really." She grimaced.

What was she supposed to say to make him understand how she felt? She'd come here because she loved him, but that didn't change her feelings about marriage. Being his mistress would empower her. It would give her the wherewithal to leave him if he ever betrayed her. The matrimonial state would strip her of her rights, her independence.

"I know you better than that," he snapped. She bit down on her lip as she met his troubled gaze.

"A few moments ago, you told me you'd do anything for me."

"Is that what this is all about?" Relief eased the lines of tension in his face. "You want me to do something for you."

"Yes. I want to be your mistress."

"*What?*" Disbelief stiffened his features, and his fingers bit painfully into her shoulders making her wince.

"It's the best solution." She flinched at the anger darkening his face.

"Best for whom?" He pushed her away from him then turned to snatch up his clothing from the floor. "*Fuck.* You came here knowing full well you had no intention of marrying me."

"No, that's not true," she cried out. The bitter accusation sliced into her heart. "I didn't plan any of this."

"What do you take me for, Julia? A fool? You said you loved me, what else was I supposed to think?" The icy note in his voice frightened her as she watched him jerk on his trousers with unrestrained violence.

"I do love you," she said quietly. Sick at heart, she continued to dress while her gaze kept track of his angry movements. She should have known he would react this way. As he shrugged into his shirt, he whipped around to face her.

"Tell me why you refuse to marry me."

"I…it's just that…I just can't be with you in that way, Morgan."

"That's not an answer and you know it," he ground out through clenched teeth.

"I told you I loved you, what more do you want? I will not give up my independence."

Defiant in the face of his anger, she tugged viciously at the laces of her corset. The man was just being stubborn. Why couldn't he be satisfied with the fact that she was willing to be with him? Admitting that she loved him had been difficult enough. She grabbed her dress up off the floor and threw it on over her head.

"I'll tell you what I want," he said in a tight voice. "I want you to love me with all your heart, not just a part of it."

"I do love you," she snapped.

"You think you love me, but if you really did, you'd trust me not to hurt you. Love involves trust, Julia. You can't have one without the other." The quiet resignation in his voice said she was losing the battle to make him understand why she refused to marry him. It shot a bolt of panic through her.

"Oh God, Morgan, I can't. Don't you understand? I can't take that sort of risk."

"Life's a risk Julia, without it there's no reward. I want all of your love, not just a piece of it. You're my passion, and if I can't have all of you, then God help me, I'll find a way to live without you." Without looking at her, he strode toward the study door and turned the key.

"Morgan please…I…you don't understand—"

"I think you know the way out." He yanked the door open so hard it protested with a loud squeal against the violence. An instant later, he was gone, taking her heart and soul with him.

Chapter 22

Storming up the stairs, Morgan reached the second floor landing and strode down the hall to the master bedroom. His anger had the force of a steam engine over its limit. The door to his room flew back from his violent rage to crack loudly against the wall. Damn her.

He paced the room, his body tense with frustration. Halting his frenzied stride, he slammed the bottom of his fist into the window frame. In the street below, he saw Julia hesitate in front of her carriage. For a split second, he held his breath as she turned back toward the front door. An instant later, she whirled about and hurried to the vehicle.

Fuck, it had *never* occurred to him that she might have the audacity to offer herself up as his mistress. He didn't want a mistress. He wanted a wife. A woman to bear his children, someone to love him in spite of his faults. Someone to grow old with. He wanted Julia.

There had been no hesitation in her when she'd performed that dance of seduction for him. She hadn't wavered in tantalizing his cock with her mouth or the rest of her delicious curves. And yet, afterward, she'd blatantly refused to commit herself. She'd been unwilling to trust him. Hell, she'd even admitted she was in love with him, but she'd stopped short at making the commitment he wanted her to make. What was it going to take to convince her that he could be trusted?

His fist thudded against the window jamb one more time before he strode to the middle of the room. One hand rubbing the back of his neck, he closed his eyes and remembered the feel of her against him. After all this time away from her, it had been like a taste of heaven to have Julia in his arms again.

Self-preservation had driven him to work nights over the past few weeks simply because he didn't think he'd be able to stay away from her if he'd seen her on a daily basis in his offices. Stress had eventually taken its toll, and he'd succumbed to a migraine. The past few days had been a living hell of pain and despair.

He'd almost given up hope she would come to him, and then she'd walked into his study on the pretense of ensuring he was well. She'd come to him. Even confessed that she loved him. How the Marlborough Set would laugh if they knew a woman had brought Morgan St. Claire to his knees.

God, the irony of it all. How many times had he had women beg him not to leave them? Beg him to love them. He'd never been cruel when breaking off an affair, but now, he fully understood the pain those women had experienced when he'd left them. Now, he was the one willing to beg. And if he thought for one moment that it would make a difference with Julia, he would gladly humble himself again. He was willing to do anything for her.

No. The one thing he wouldn't do was keep her as his mistress. What he wanted was Julia's full heart. She loved him, but he wanted her to trust him too. Being his mistress would make it far too easy for her to walk away from him the moment her fear took over.

What the hell was he going to do? Worse yet, what was he to do with this monstrosity of a house? The empty silence of it tugged at him with a wrenching ache. Both hands clutched the back of his head as he stared down at the floor. When she'd come through his study door, it had taken every inch of will power he possessed not to pull her into his arms and overwhelm her senses with lovemaking. But he'd promised himself to let her choose. He just never thought he could lose her. Living without Julia was going to be harder than anything he'd ever done before in his life.

His gut tightened with emotion and he knew the only remedy for dealing with his pain was work. He'd work until he'd driven her out of his head, out of his blood. He'd work until he was numb from everything. The numbness would take away this ache inside him. With a grunt, he strode out of the bedroom to go to the office. There at least he could keep his mind focused on something other than Julia.

The woman in the portrait smiled at her. A self-satisfied, confident smile. Glaring at the painting, she turned away from the artwork and started to pace the floor of her bedroom. Why couldn't she be like that woman? She wanted to, but she didn't know how. No, that wasn't true. She'd been that bold, seductive woman in Morgan's study more than two weeks ago. It still amazed her how audacious she'd been in her efforts to seduce him. But how to be the woman in the portrait wasn't the problem, what she lacked was the courage to be that woman.

She was a fool. Her refusal to marry Morgan was the worst decision she'd ever made. Choice hadn't been an issue when she married Oscar. Her mother had seen to that. But Morgan was different, she could have agreed to his marriage proposal if she'd only had the fortitude to do so. He'd said he wanted her trust, and she wanted desperately to give that to him. She simply didn't know how.

The sound of the doorbell echoed softly through her room. Unable to help herself, she raced out into the upstairs hall. When she reached the top of the steps, she struggled to keep her disappointment from showing as she met Catherine's arched look.

"Well that's a fine look to greet me with," her cousin said with a bite of humor. "I take it you were hoping to see someone else."

"No, not exactly…I just thought—oh it's not important." Julia waited for Catherine to climb the stairs then led the way into the upstairs salon.

"You thought I was Morgan St. Claire." Catherine's statement made Julia jerk her head around to eye her cousin.

"I did not." Ignoring the protest, Catherine swept across the room to the fireplace. As she tugged off her gloves in precise movements, she gave Julia a stern look.

"Do not treat me like I'm an addle–brained halfwit. You were hoping St. Claire was charging up those stairs to whisk you away."

"Now you're being ridiculous." Julia waved her hand at her cousin in a dismissive gesture.

"No, that would be *your* forte, my dear." Catherine shook her finger at her. "I thought you had more backbone than this."

"Even if I found the courage to do something, it's too late now. He doesn't want me anymore." Julia averted her gaze from the disappointment in her cousin's eyes.

"How do you know that?"

"I just do. Our last parting was far from amicable." She flinched at the memory of Morgan's icy anger as he stood at the door of his study telling her to see herself out. The claw marks on her heart still lay open and bleeding from that moment.

"Well, it would seem St. Claire has forgotten about that little misunderstanding." Catherine sent her a triumphant look. "I saw the man this morning on Rotten Row, and what do you think the first thing out of his mouth was? It was to ask about you."

The declaration made her heart leap, and she turned away from Catherine to hide the hope she knew had to be lighting her face. He'd asked about her. Even despite his anger, he'd inquired as to how she was. Alarm shot through her. Oh God—Catherine was not known for her discretion, but rather for her blunt speech. Whirling back around, she scowled at her cousin.

"What did you tell him? If you told him I was pining away for him, Catherine, I shall…I shall make certain Lord Greyling finds out about that little tryst you had with Lord Dunham last year."

"Rubbish," Catherine half snorted with disgust, "It was hardly a tryst, and I couldn't care less what Lord Greyling thinks."

Julia frowned in puzzlement at the blithe statement. Of course Catherine cared what Greyling thought of her. There was a long history between the two, and her cousin's cavalier response surprised her. Had something happened between the couple?

"But I thought you and he—"

"Don't you dare try to change the subject." Consternation flashed in the other woman's eyes, but she didn't give Julia time to interrupt. "This conversation is about you and how you're going to resolve this matter with St. Claire. It's high time you go after the man."

"That's impossible," Julia snapped.

"Nothing's impossible. Go to him."

"I can't," she said with a vehement shake of her head. Catherine crossed the room and wrapped an arm around Julia's shoulders.

"What is it you're afraid of, dearest?"

The gentle quiet of her closest confidant's voice made her swallow a hot knot inside her throat. Closing her eyes, Julia stifled the tears threatening to spill down her cheeks.

"I'm afraid of loving him so much that I'll lose myself. The person who I am."

"Is your life now—without him—better than loving him so much you forget where he ends and you begin?" Catherine's softly worded question tightened the vise around her heart.

Over the past two weeks, she'd suffered more torment and pain than anything Oscar had ever inflicted on her. Her body, mind, and soul cried out for Morgan every waking minute. Life had become bleak and dark. It was as bad, if not worse, than when she was suffering the bedevilment of her late husband. And now, Catherine had reminded her of Morgan's words. Life was a risk. Without it, there was no reward.

Those words were the key to her happiness. Convincing Morgan she trusted him had to be demonstrated with action. Words would no longer work as he would always question her decision. Maybe not openly, but it would always be between them. There was only one way she could make him understand that no matter what the risk, she was willing to do anything just to be with him. The question was whether or not she had the courage to go through with it. Turning her head, the empathy in Catherine's eyes reassured her.

"Did Morgan say what his plans were over the next few days?" At the question, Catherine's mouth curved with a conspiratorial smile and nodded.

"He did, indeed. Shall we formulate your plan of attack?"

Filled with fear, and yet a delicious anticipation, Julia nodded. Soon she would know whether or not her gamble would reap the love and happiness with Morgan she so desperately wanted.

Chapter 23

Morgan wearily entered the darkened house, closing the front door behind him. Rolling his head in a half circle, he attempted to relieve some of the tension in his neck. He paused briefly to turn up the gaslight in the foyer then moved on into the study. The small fire in the hearth was the only light illuminating the room. It was a sight he was growing accustomed too.

The day after Julia had left the house, he gone to work hoping she'd be there, but she wasn't. She hadn't been to the shipping office at all. In the days that followed, his life had taken on a familiar pattern. After a twelve to thirteen-hour day, he came back to an empty house and a cold supper Mrs. Welkins always had ready for him. The remainder of his evening was spent morosely pondering his fate over several glasses of alcohol.

Morgan stoked the fire then walked to the liquor cabinet and pulled out a decanter of whiskey. How he ever thought work would push Julia out of his head was beyond his comprehension. Despite his best efforts to bury himself in work, thoughts of her continuously filled his head. He should have agreed to keep her as his mistress. At least she'd be with him now. But that hadn't satisfied him. Instead, he'd pigheadedly demanded more. Asking for more than she could give. Even now, the memory of her touch and scent, made him ache. His cock stiffened and pressed against his stomach.

"Damn it to hell," he muttered as he splashed a generous portion of liquor into a glass.

The decanter top rattled as he dropped the stopper back into the container's neck. With a jerk, he tossed the whiskey down his throat in one deep gulp. He welcomed the fire that burned its way to his stomach. It was a reflection of the pain ripping him apart inside.

Eager to occupy his head with something other than thoughts of Julia, he took the decanter and glass over to his desk. With a flick of his wrist, he turned up the flame on the lamp sitting at one corner of the workspace. Shrugging out of his jacket, he tugged his thin ribbon of a tie off his neck and undid the first few buttons of his shirt.

He grunted with weariness as he threw himself into his chair. From his seat, he stared at the messages stacked neatly on the desktop. On top of the stack, he recognized a note from Mrs. Welkins. Listlessly, he lifted the folded missive off the top of the stack and opened it.

Mr. St. Claire,

A courier delivered a package for you just before I left. The instructions were to place it in your bedroom, and I have left it there for you. I also left a cold supper for you in the kitchen.

Regards, Mrs. Welkins

He tossed the note to one side and leaned forward to pull the whiskey decanter toward him. Another liberal bout of liquor filled his glass. This time though, he only drank half of what he poured. What sort of package was upstairs in his room? He couldn't remember ordering anything that required delivery to this mausoleum. Picking up the note again, he studied his housekeeper's writing as he took another drink from his glass.

With a frown, he got to his feet. If the woman had wanted to pique his interest, she'd done so. He was curious to find out what was in this mysterious package. His glass thudded softly against the top of the desk as he set it down and moved out into the foyer to climb the stairs. Walking down the hall toward his room, he snorted in disgust. He should have brought the whiskey decanter and his glass with him. It was just as easy to get drunk in his room as the study. At least he could have wound up in bed instead of the uncomfortable chair at the fireplace. He pushed open the door to his bedroom and froze.

"Christ Jesus."

He was dreaming. Nothing else could explain the exquisite picture in front of him. She was the portrait come to life. Reclined against a bed of navy blue pillows trimmed in gold, Julia was a feast for his eyes. The first and only time he'd seen the painting, he'd memorized every little nuance, every colorful detail, but none of what he remembered matched this erotic picture.

Candles filled the room, and their light reflected the auburn tints in her hair. Just as in the painting, her hair draped over one shoulder to cover one breast and leaving the other exposed. God she was beautiful. In the candlelight, her skin possessed a golden hue, and it beckoned him like a siren.

The nipples on her firm breasts were already rigid, ready for his mouth to tease. Her hand rested on her softly rounded belly, and it made him want to touch her there. No, he wanted to touch her everywhere. Bloody hell. He wanted to fuck her until he was exhausted, and then he wanted to fuck her again.

Even from where he stood, he could smell the tart lemony scent of her. His gaze slid downward to the triangle of wiry curls just below her hand. He suddenly realized it was impossible to swallow when one's mouth was dry. God almighty. What the hell was she doing here? Was this another way to torture him? If she thought to come in here and tease him simply for her own pleasure, then she could leave before he even touched her.

But God, how he wanted to touch her. His cock hardened and throbbed a desperate signal to him. He ignored it. Folding his arms across his chest, his fingers dug viciously into his biceps. It was a struggle to keep his aroused state under control as he cleared his throat and fought to find his voice.

"What are you doing here, Julia?" Hell, his voice sounded like he was suffering from a sore throat. The small smile curling her mouth upward on one side said she knew just how the sight of her was affecting him.

"You told me once that you wanted to see the woman in the portrait in your bed."

She stretched out her hand to him as she spoke. With great difficulty, he suppressed the urge to go to her, and his fingers bit even deeper into his arm. Damn it, he wanted to know what game she was playing. She'd done this to him once before, and he wasn't willing to go through that hell again.

"I seem to recall you telling me the woman in that painting didn't exist."

The smile on her lips disappeared, and a shadow darkened her gaze until the hazel color blended into a mossy green. Her expression grew troubled as she sat up straight. The movement sent a lock of hair tumbling down over a shoulder to curl around one nipple. He suppressed an achy groan at the sight.

"I didn't think she existed either, but you showed me how to be the woman you want."

"That still doesn't explain why you're here." The harsh statement made her flinch, but she didn't retreat.

"I'm here because I love you, Morgan. I'll be your mistress, I'll marry you, I'll do whatever you want, but I can't live without you."

There, she'd said the words. Made her declaration. What would he do? Julia sucked in a sharp breath as she watched and waited for him to say something. Anything. He stood still as a statue as he studied her. It was impossible to read his thoughts, and she trembled as she realized he might very well reject her. His eyes narrowed as he arched an eyebrow.

"If you think to make a fool of me a second time, Julia, you're mistaken."

"I'm the one who's been the fool. I don't blame you for not believing me, but would you at least give me a chance to prove my sincerity?" She searched his expression for some inkling as to his thoughts, but he was closed off from her. The realization made every one of her nerve endings scream from the tension.

"If all I wanted was for you to satisfy my unruly cock, Julia, I would never have proposed marriage. You didn't trust me to love you, so tell me why I should trust you now?" The bitterness in his voice tore at her heart. She'd hurt him. Badly. It was evident from the harsh twist of his lips.

"I knew you might think that. I knew there was only one way to prove that I trust you implicitly." Swallowing the tiny ball of fear in her throat, she reminded herself that this was Morgan. The man she loved. A man who'd declared his love for her time and time again. Slowly, she reclined back onto the bed and reached for the black silk tie she'd knotted to the headboard earlier.

The implacable expression on his face disappeared as she slid her hands into the noose she'd created and grasping the end of the tie with her teeth she pulled it snug around her wrists. The horror in his gaze reassured her that she had made the right choice. In three long strides, he was at the headboard, his hands reaching for the silk strap that bound her to his bed. With a vehement shake of her head, she stopped him.

"Morgan, *no!*"

Staring up at him, she saw the rapid rise and fall of his chest as his eyes fixated on her bound wrists. The tension in him was visible to the naked eye. She saw a muscle flex in his cheek as he swallowed hard. Her gaze drifted downward to where his erection was stiff and hard, his trousers stretched tight across his arousal. He was hot and excited. She could tell by the way he held himself rigid. She looked up at him, but he averted his gaze in a manner that told her he was appalled at being so aroused by the sight of her.

"Don't do this, sweetheart," he rasped. She swallowed again, but this time with something akin to anticipation.

"I need to prove how much I trust you. Not just to you, but to myself as well."

"Christ Jesus, Julia." He shoved a hand through his hair, the movement taut with mixed emotions. "You're asking me to make you relive—"

"*No!* No, I'm asking you to make love to me, Morgan."

What her husband had done to her had nothing to do with love. But when Morgan touched her, there was no pain, only tenderness, passion, and love. She met his eyes steadily, hoping he could see how much she trusted him. Inside her chest, her heart raced with a bevy of emotions she couldn't separate. Desire, fear, and love mingled together in one consuming blaze that sped through her veins until her body was hot with need.

Silently protesting with a sharp shake of his head, he stared down at her for a long tense moment. Raw passion and desire burned in his eyes as she watched him struggle to control his aroused state. His reluctance told her everything she needed to know. This wonderful, passionate man loved her. He'd never hurt her. Because of his love she could vanquish all the demons Oscar had tortured her with over the years.

"Just this once, my love," she pleaded softly. "Do this for me. For us. I don't want anything between us."

"Damnation, I…" His voice faded into nothing as his fiery gaze swept over the length of her. He looked as if he could devour her from where he stood.

"It excites you?" The breathy sound of her voice surprised her, and she realized she was excited too.

"God yes. I cannot begin to tell you how hot it makes me."

"Then show me," she whispered as her eyes locked with his.

A dark groan broke from him as he pressed one knee into the bed and bent over her to capture her lips with his. The fiery hunger in his kiss echoed the craving pulling at her insides. Without the use of her hands, she couldn't pull him closer so she lifted her head to return his kiss with equal passion.

Her mouth parted beneath his and she teased her tongue across his lips. His sharp intake of breath allowed her tongue to dance with his as he deepened their kiss. There was the sharp taste of whiskey in his mouth, and she breathed in the faint scent of bergamot. God, she wanted him. Never had her need for him been this intense, this compelling.

Slowly, he sank down onto the mattress beside her, his hands sliding across her skin in gentle exploration. The soft lawn of his shirt tickled her breasts as he pressed her into the bed. Gently he tugged on her lower lip as he brushed the lower half of his body across her stomach in a suggestive act.

She was melting. It was the only way she could describe it. Need circulated in her blood like a raging fever. Without thinking, she tried to reach for him, but the tie holding her hands didn't give way. This was what she'd wanted. A way to prove to him how much she loved him. Trusted him. But it was also maddening not being able to touch him.

The hard length of him rubbed over the top of her thigh and a pleasurable ache tightened her sex. Writhing beneath him, she whimpered at the desire growing inside her. His mouth feathered kisses across the ridge of her shoulder, and she gasped when the rough pad of his thumb caressed one nipple.

At the heated touch, she arched her back, pressing her breast into the cup of his hand. Her submissive movement drew a sharp hiss of excitement from him, and his mouth streaked across her skin to find the hard peak. The moment his lips clamped down on her nipple, fire sped across her skin, and she moaned with pleasure. While he suckled her, strong fingers trailed a path downward over his skin until his palm pressed against the apex of her thighs.

Heat streaked through her and another moan escaped her as she moved her hips in an attempt to have him touch her more intimately. Dear Lord, in all the moments they'd been together this one was the most potent yet. Bound to the bed, she knew she was completely at his mercy, and yet she wasn't afraid. It was the most freeing experience she'd ever known.

His fingers stroked the inside of her thigh, teasing her with a feather light caress over her curls before drawing back. It made her body taut with need, and she shifted her hips again in an effort to make him touch her.

"Oh God, please…please, Morgan. I need you to touch me."

"How do you want me to touch you, sweetheart?" His finger parted her slick folds and rubbed over the sensitive nub of flesh inside. She immediately bucked against his touch, and his voice grew raspy. "Like this?"

"Oh yes. God yes," she cried out with pleasure as he slid his finger in and out of her.

Numb to everything but the pleasure of his touch, she thrust her hips upward to match his erotic strokes. A moment later, she was suddenly deprived of his touch. She moaned her protest as he slid off the bed and removed his clothing. With deliberate slowness, he undressed in front of her. Naked before her, he grabbed his rock hard erection and stroked himself.

"Is this what you want, sweetheart? Do you want to feel me filling you, driving into you until you come all over this hard cock of mine?"

She gasped in shock at the coarse words. Unable to reply, she watched in fascination as he stroked himself in an almost languid fashion. Aroused to a fevered pitch, silk tightened around her wrists as she arched her body upward in a display of wanton need. God she wanted him. Needed to feel him inside her, loving her until they climaxed together.

She tugged at her bindings, not in apprehension, but anticipation. The realization made her go still, and she shuddered as her gaze flickered upward to meet the desire flaring in his blue eyes. It was a passion born of love. His love had broken the chains that had held her prisoner for so long. There was no more fear, only the overwhelming need to love and be loved in every way imaginable.

"For the love of god, Morgan," she whispered hoarsely. "Can't you see how much I love you? Want you? Need..."

"What do you need, my love?" The endearment squeezed at her heart as she watched him smear a bead of white fluid over the cap of his stiff erection. Her eyes met his, and she drew in a ragged breath.

"I need...your cock inside me. I'm yours completely. Do what you wish with me."

She'd just offered herself up to him in a way that illustrated the consummate trust she'd placed in him. Her words gave him permission to take her in any way he liked, but all he wanted to do was pleasure her until she clenched at his cock and milked him dry.

Laying on the bed before him, tied like a supplicant offered up to the gods, she had to be the most erotic vision he'd ever seen. She was submitting herself to him in a manner that made him hotter than he'd ever been for any woman in his life.

There was no fear in her gaze, only desire. Christ Jesus, he needed to feel her wrapped around him, her muscles squeezing him with exquisite tightness. He reached out to run his hand over a long, silky leg. A soft sound escaped her at his touch, and he smiled down at her.

Slowly, so as not to frighten her, he moved his body over hers until his erection pressed lightly against her curls. Agitated, she squirmed beneath him in an effort to make him penetrate her. He resisted, but barely. With her eyes closed, she was the most beautifully erotic woman he'd ever seen.

A part of him struggled with taking her like this. It was the most incredible gift anyone had ever given him, and yet…he swallowed hard. He couldn't do it. He refused to take her in the same fashion her husband had done.

"Look at me," he growled. As her eyes flew open, he reached up and tugged the black silk away from her hands. "I'm not that bastard you married, and I don't need any further confirmation that you love me. Do you understand?"

"But, I wanted to prove—"

"You demonstrated it the moment you tied yourself to my bed," he rasped as he slowly pressed his cock into her. "I'm never going to let you go, Julia. You're mine. Now and for always."

"Now and for always," she repeated his pledge in a poignant whisper.

In his next breath, she released a wild cry of ecstasy the moment he thrust hard and deep into her slick folds. God, but she was tight. Desire and love glowed in her gaze as he repeated his stroke. It was like having a velvet vise wrapped around him. With an ever-increasing rhythm, he buried himself in the hot friction of her creamy folds.

Seconds later, an expression of rapture warmed her face as his name flew from her lips, and she shattered around his cock. The intensity of her rippling contractions tugged at him with increasing pressure until with one last thrust, he exploded inside her. For a long moment, he shuddered against her, reveling in the sweet aftermath of their lovemaking. With a final throb inside her hot depths, he rolled onto his side and pulled her with him.

A tremor lanced through Julia as she buried her face into Morgan's chest. The silence between them was warm and drowsy as she breathed in the hot earthy scent of him. Happiness and love swelled inside her. He'd given her not only his heart, but her freedom as well. Without Morgan's love, she would never have been able to escape the demons of self-doubt that Oscar had instilled in her. More than that, she'd overcome her deepest fears to show Morgan how much she loved him.

His mouth brushed her forehead, and she tilted her head back to smile at him. The somber expression on his face stifled her happiness. Something was wrong. Had she failed to make him understand why she'd chosen to do what she'd done?

"Morgan, I—"

A warm finger pressed against her lips. "Shhh. It's all right. I was simply thinking how precious a gift you've just given me. Why did you do it?"

Her hand came up to hold his, and she kissed his palm. "I needed to make sure you understood I trust you implicitly."

"Your coming here of your own accord was more than enough, sweetheart." His arm tightened around her in a protective manner. It made her feel safe.

"No," she murmured as she looked away from him. "I needed to destroy the demons Oscar left behind. I did it for me as much as I did it for you."

"And are they gone?" Despite the nonchalance of the question, she could hear the concern in his voice.

"Yes." Her gaze returned to his face as she smiled. "I should have listened when you told me that there were no rewards without risk."

"And you've realized the error of your ways." The light teasing note to his voice made her tap him lightly on his chest.

"You're far too arrogant, Morgan St. Claire."

"Perhaps, but I'm deeply in love, which brings us to the subject of marriage." His gaze was intent as he searched her features. "Tomorrow, I intend to find someone to marry us, and until we're married, you're not leaving my sight."

"I promise I won't run this time." She caressed his cheek, and he turned his head to kiss the inside of her palm.

"I know that sweetheart, but I'm not willing to give you the chance to have second thoughts. Besides, I can't think of anything more pleasurable than spending the rest of the night and early morning, making love to you."

Sighing, she nestled her cheek against his shoulder, content to remain there forever. The thought of the portrait flitted into her head. Had she really succeeded in becoming the woman Morgan had seen in the portrait, or was she only a figment of their imagination? With a quick movement, she forced Morgan onto his back and straddled him. Her hands braced on the bed above his shoulders, she leaned toward him.

"Tell me, St. Claire. This portrait you saw some time ago. Does the woman really exist or is she a figment of your imagination?"

Lowering her head, she brushed her lips lightly over his, and she immediately felt his arousal pressing into her leg. Julia lifted her head to stare down at him. Flames flickered in the depths of his dark gaze, and a seductive smile curled his lips.

"Yes, she's quite real. In fact, I'm certain I can retire my handkerchiefs for good," he said as his smile became a wicked grin.

"An excellent idea, because I'm the last affair you'll ever have, Morgan St. Claire." Slowly, and with a sigh of happiness, she lowered her head and proceeded to show him exactly why.

Other Titles by Monica Burns

THE RECKLESS ROCKWOODS SERIES
Obsession, Book 1
Dangerous, Book 2, Award-Winner
The Highlander's Woman, Book 3
Redemption, Book 4
The Beastly Duke, Book 5

THE RECKLESS ROCKWOODS NOVELS
The Rogue's Offer, Book 1
The Rogue's Countess, Book 2

SELF-MADE MEN SERIES
His To Command, Book 1 (Novella)
His Mistress, Book 2

FOREVERMORE SERIES
Forever Mine, International Award-Winner, Book 1
Forever Yours, Book 2
Forever My Lass, Book 3 (Coming 01/23)

STAND ALONE
Kismet
Mirage, Award Winner
Pleasure Me, Award Winner
Love's Portrait
Love's Revenge
A Bluestocking Christmas
His for the Holidays

About The Author

Monica Burns is a bestselling author of spicy historical, contemporary, and paranormal romance. She penned her first romance at the age of nine when she selected the pseudonym she uses today. From the days when she hid her stories from her sisters to her first completed full-length manuscript, she always believed in her dream despite rejections and setbacks. Monica is a survivor who believes every hero and heroine deserves a HEA (Happily Ever After), especially if she's writing the story.

Her multiple book awards include FOREVER MINE chosen as a 2015 Must Read by USA Today HEA Blog, a Gold medal from International Book Awards, and an IPPY Bronze medal. Other awards include the 2011 RT BookReviews Reviewers Choice Award and the 2012 Gayle Wilson Heart of Excellence Award for Pleasure Me. She is also the recipient of the prestigious PRISM Best of the Best award for her paranormal romance Assassin's Heart.

www.ingramcontent.com/pod-product-compliance
Lightning Source LLC
Chambersburg PA
CBHW070501200726
48293CB00007B/2319